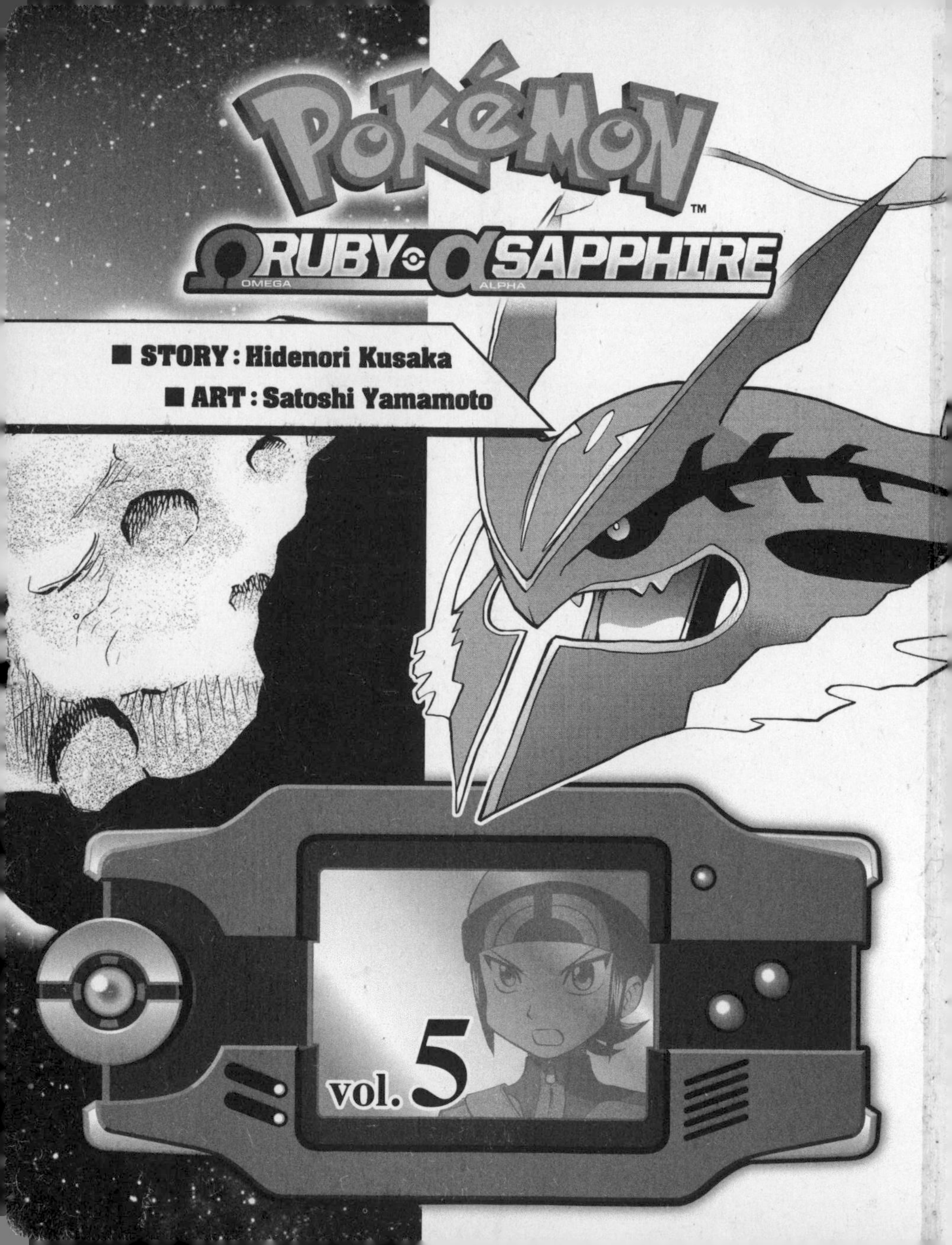
POKÉMON™
ΩRUBY αSAPPHIRE
OMEGA ALPHA
■ STORY : Hidenori Kusaka
■ ART : Satoshi Yamamoto
vol. 5

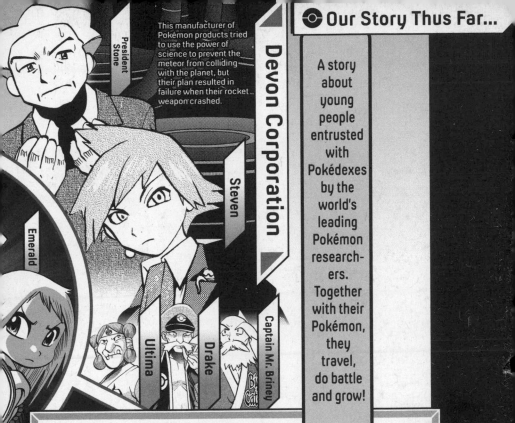

Our Story Thus Far...

A story about young people entrusted with Pokédexes by the world's leading Pokémon research-ers. Together with their Pokémon, they travel, do battle and grow!

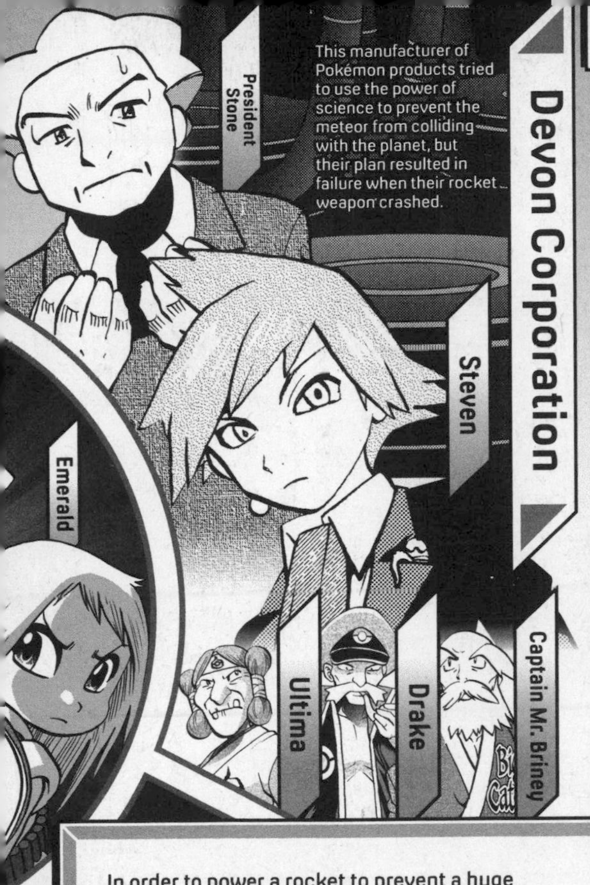

Devon Corporation
President Stone
This manufacturer of Pokémon products tried to use the power of science to prevent the meteor from colliding with the planet, but their plan resulted in failure when their rocket weapon crashed.
Steven
Emerald
Captain Mr. Briney
Drake
Ultima

In order to power a rocket to prevent a huge approaching meteor from striking the planet, Steven Stone, president of the Devon Corporation, summons the three Pokédex holders of Hoenn to help him convert the life force of many Pokémon into Infinity Energy.

The rocket launch ends in failure due to sabotage by Zinnia, the Lorekeeper of the Draconid People. The Draconid have long predicted the arrival of the meteor and claim they know how to prevent it from striking the planet. During the battle with Zinnia, Sapphire mysteriously goes missing.

Ruby and Emerald are hit by the shockwave when Legendary Pokémon Groudon and Kyogre suddenly appear. Our heroes regain consciousness at Meteor Falls, where the Elder of the Draconid People provides them with clues to saving the world. Armed with new information, Ruby and his father head for Johto in search of Legendary Pokémon Rayquaza. Will they find Rayquaza and help it master its move, Dragon Ascent? They're about to run out of time...!

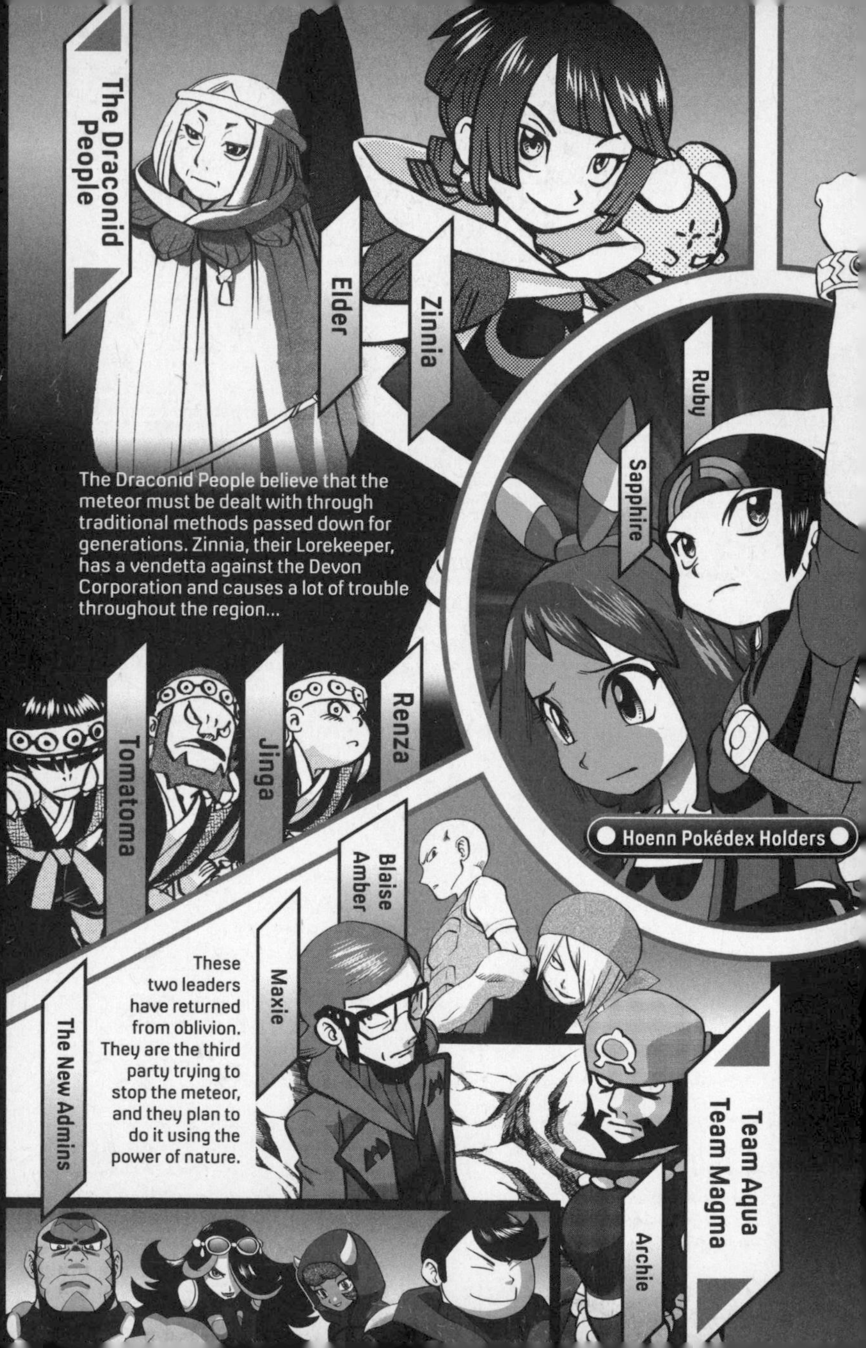
Zinnia
Elder
The Draconid People
The Draconid People believe that the meteor must be dealt with through traditional methods passed down for generations. Zinnia, their Lorekeeper, has a vendetta against the Devon Corporation and causes a lot of trouble throughout the region...
Ruby
Sapphire
Hoenn Pokédex Holders
Renza
Jinga
Tomatoma
Team Aqua
Team Magma
Archie
Maxie
Blaise
Amber
These two leaders have returned from oblivion. They are the third party trying to stop the meteor, and they plan to do it using the power of nature.
The New Admins

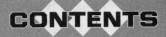

CONTENTS

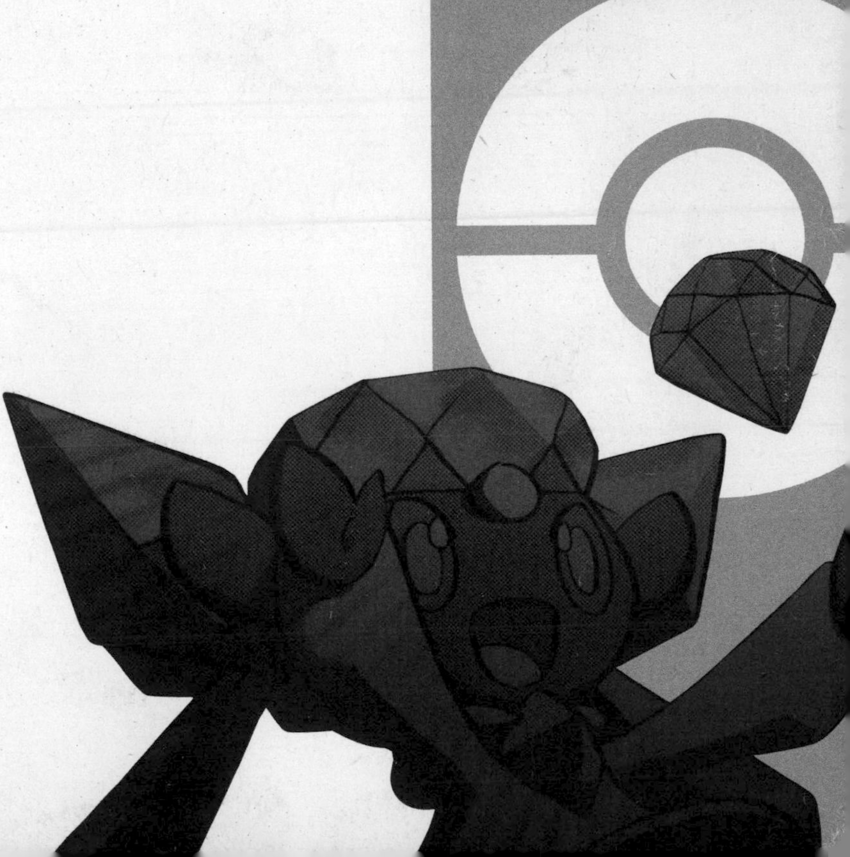

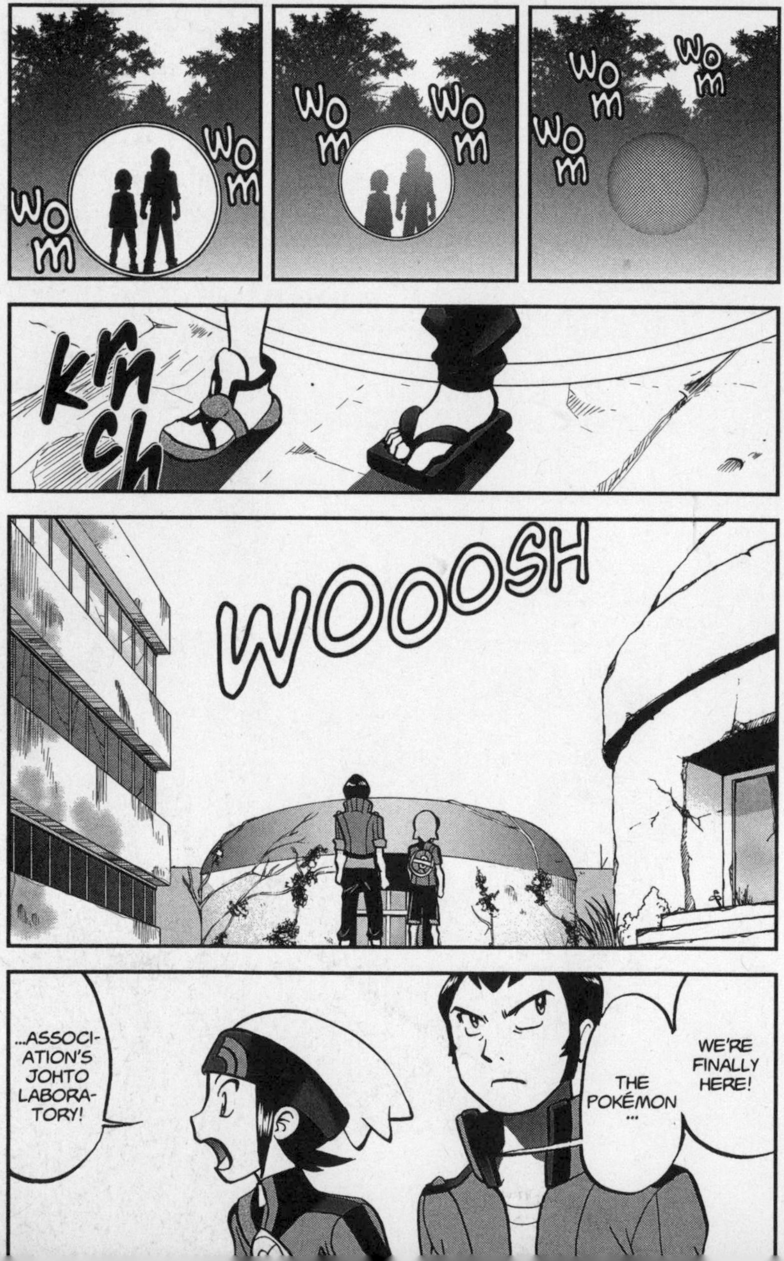
wom
wom
wom
wom
wom
wom
wom
krnch
WOOOSH
WE'RE FINALLY HERE!
THE POKÉMON…
…ASSOCIATION'S JOHTO LABORATORY!

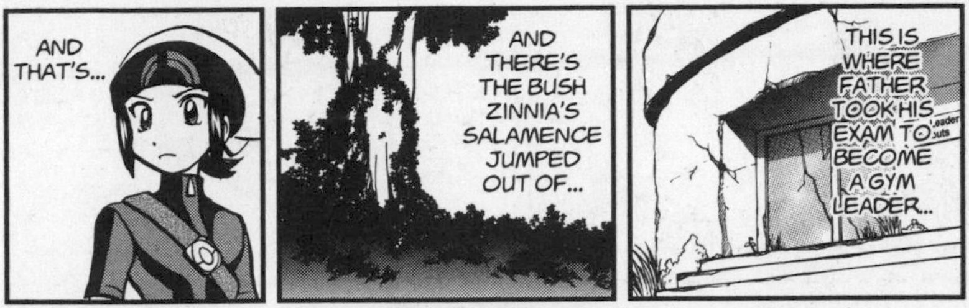
THIS IS WHERE FATHER TOOK HIS EXAM TO BECOME A GYM LEADER...
AND THERE'S THE BUSH ZINNIA'S SALAMENCE JUMPED OUT OF...
AND THAT'S...

Omega Alpha Adventure 15

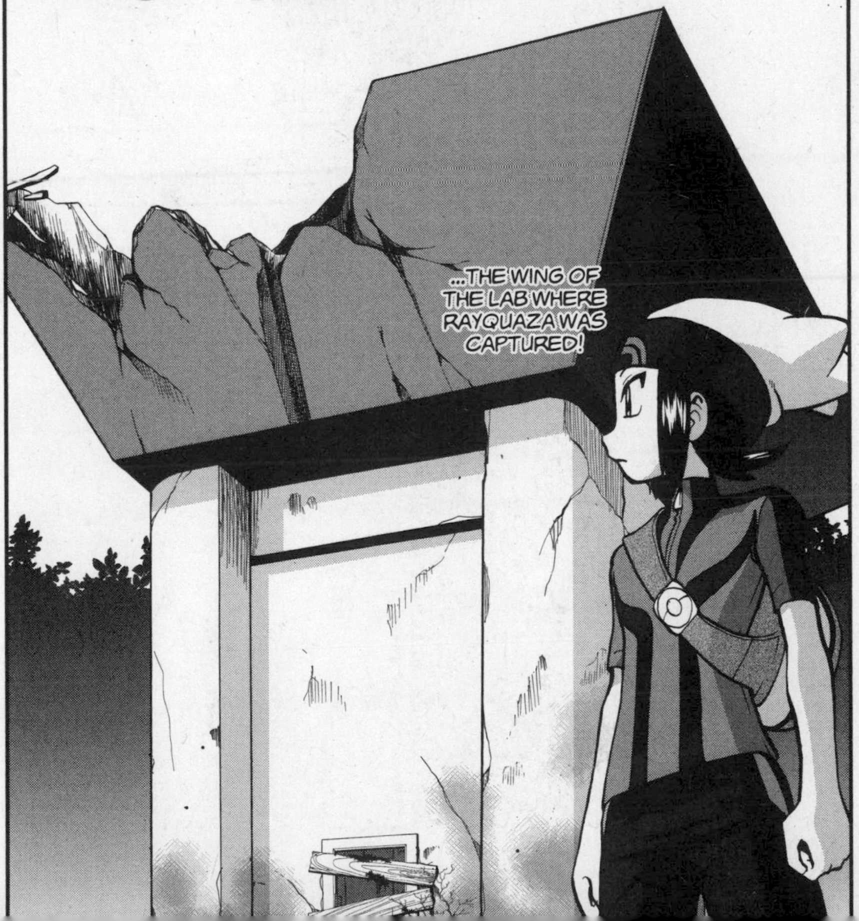
...THE WING OF THE LAB WHERE RAYQUAZA WAS CAPTURED!

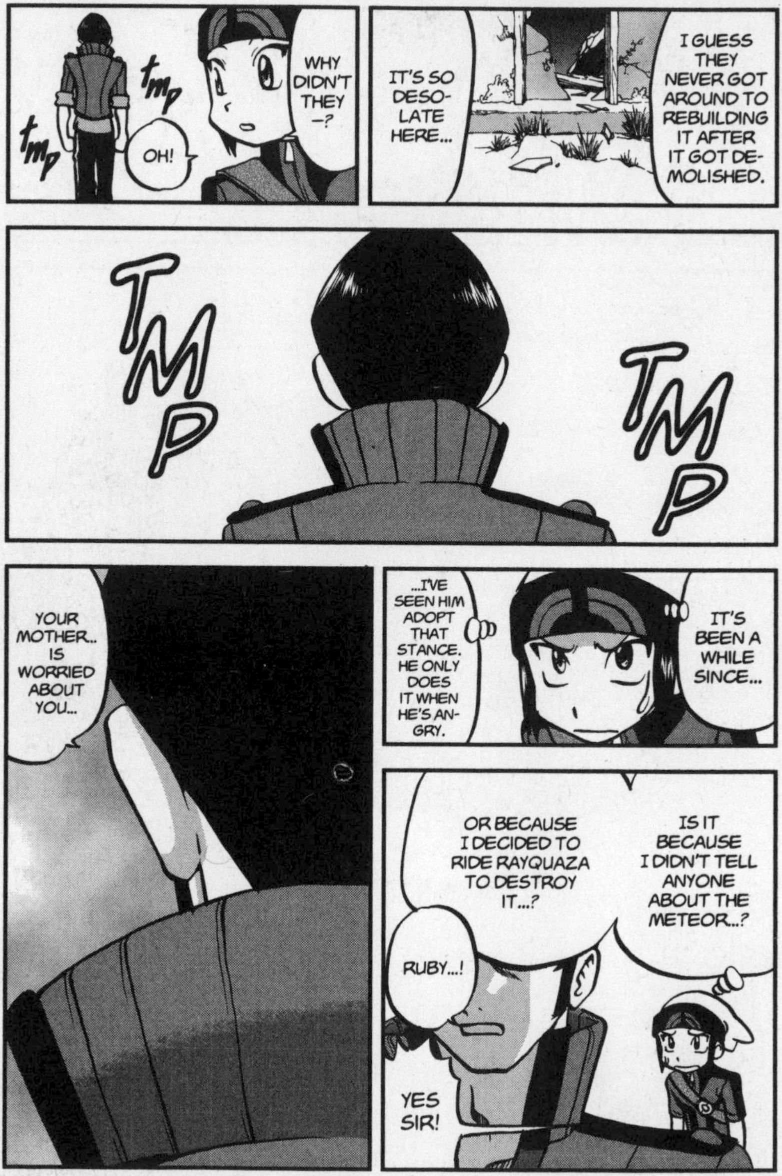
I GUESS THEY NEVER GOT AROUND TO REBUILDING IT AFTER IT GOT DEMOLISHED.
IT'S SO DESOLATE HERE...
WHY DIDN'T THEY —?
tmp
tmp
OH!
TMP
TMP
IT'S BEEN A WHILE SINCE...
...I'VE SEEN HIM ADOPT THAT STANCE. HE ONLY DOES IT WHEN HE'S ANGRY.
IS IT BECAUSE I DIDN'T TELL ANYONE ABOUT THE METEOR...?
OR BECAUSE I DECIDED TO RIDE RAYQUAZA TO DESTROY IT...?
RUBY...!
YES SIR!
YOUR MOTHER.. IS WORRIED ABOUT YOU...

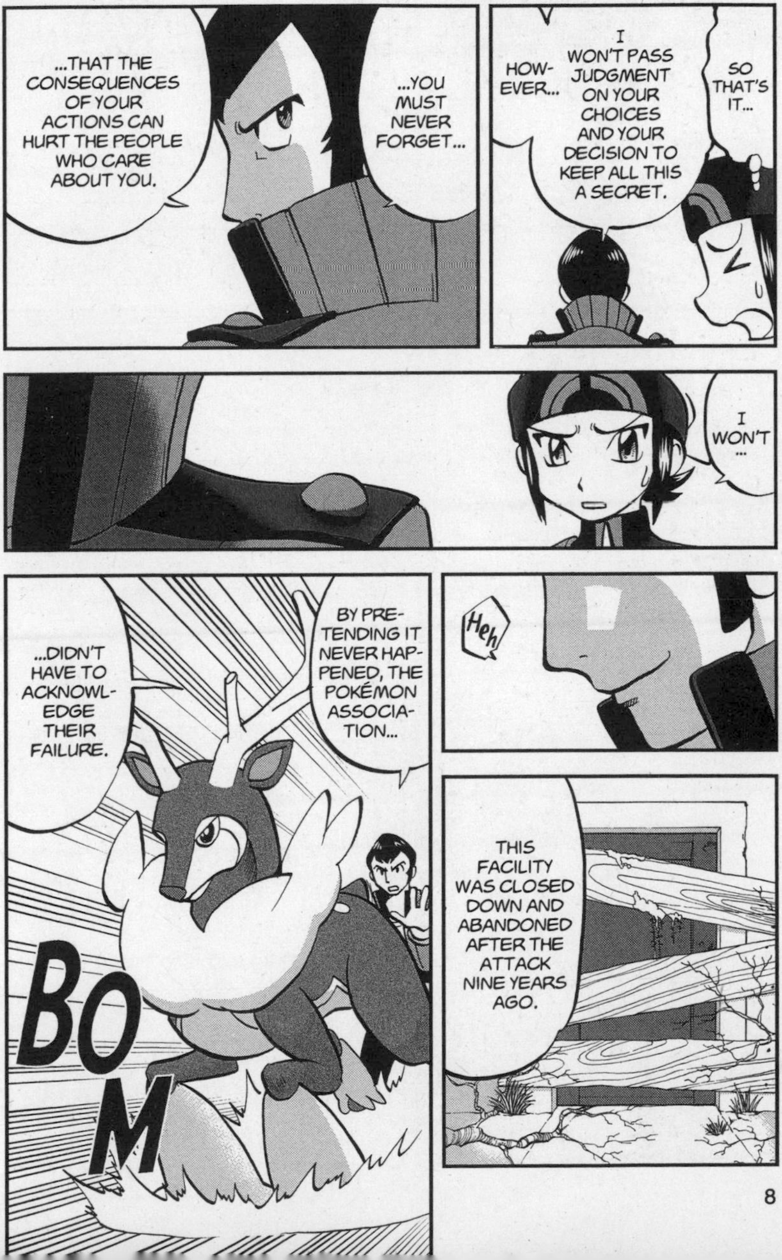
SO THAT'S IT...
I WON'T PASS JUDGMENT ON YOUR CHOICES AND YOUR DECISION TO KEEP ALL THIS A SECRET.
HOW-EVER...
...YOU MUST NEVER FORGET...
...THAT THE CONSEQUENCES OF YOUR ACTIONS CAN HURT THE PEOPLE WHO CARE ABOUT YOU.
I WON'T...
Heh
THIS FACILITY WAS CLOSED DOWN AND ABANDONED AFTER THE ATTACK NINE YEARS AGO.
BY PRE-TENDING IT NEVER HAP-PENED, THE POKÉMON ASSOCIA-TION...
...DIDN'T HAVE TO ACKNOWL-EDGE THEIR FAILURE.
BOOM

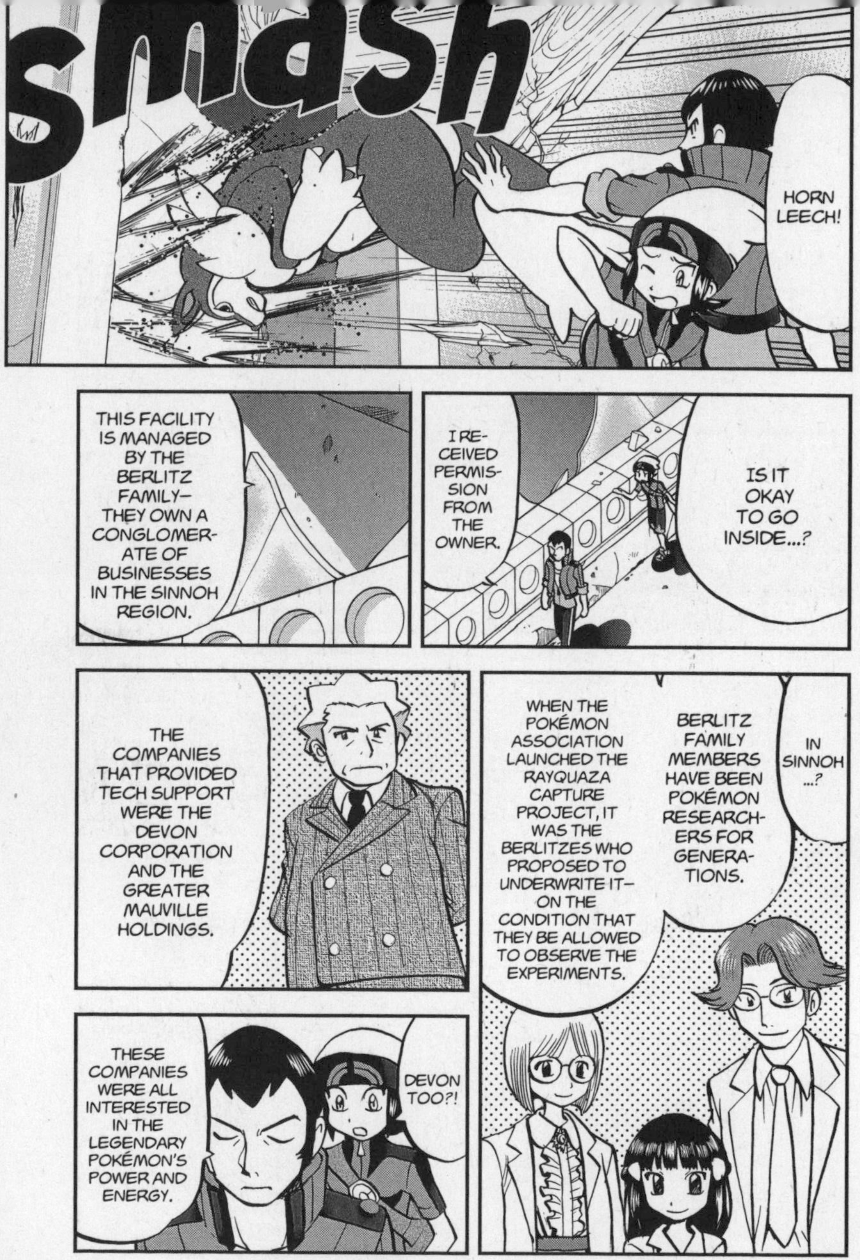
smash
HORN LEECH!
IS IT OKAY TO GO INSIDE...?
I RECEIVED PERMISSION FROM THE OWNER.
THIS FACILITY IS MANAGED BY THE BERLITZ FAMILY—THEY OWN A CONGLOMERATE OF BUSINESSES IN THE SINNOH REGION.
IN SINNOH ...?
BERLITZ FAMILY MEMBERS HAVE BEEN POKÉMON RESEARCHERS FOR GENERATIONS.
WHEN THE POKÉMON ASSOCIATION LAUNCHED THE RAYQUAZA CAPTURE PROJECT, IT WAS THE BERLITZES WHO PROPOSED TO UNDERWRITE IT—ON THE CONDITION THAT THEY BE ALLOWED TO OBSERVE THE EXPERIMENTS.
THE COMPANIES THAT PROVIDED TECH SUPPORT WERE THE DEVON CORPORATION AND THE GREATER MAUVILLE HOLDINGS.
DEVON TOO?!
THESE COMPANIES WERE ALL INTERESTED IN THE LEGENDARY POKÉMON'S POWER AND ENERGY.

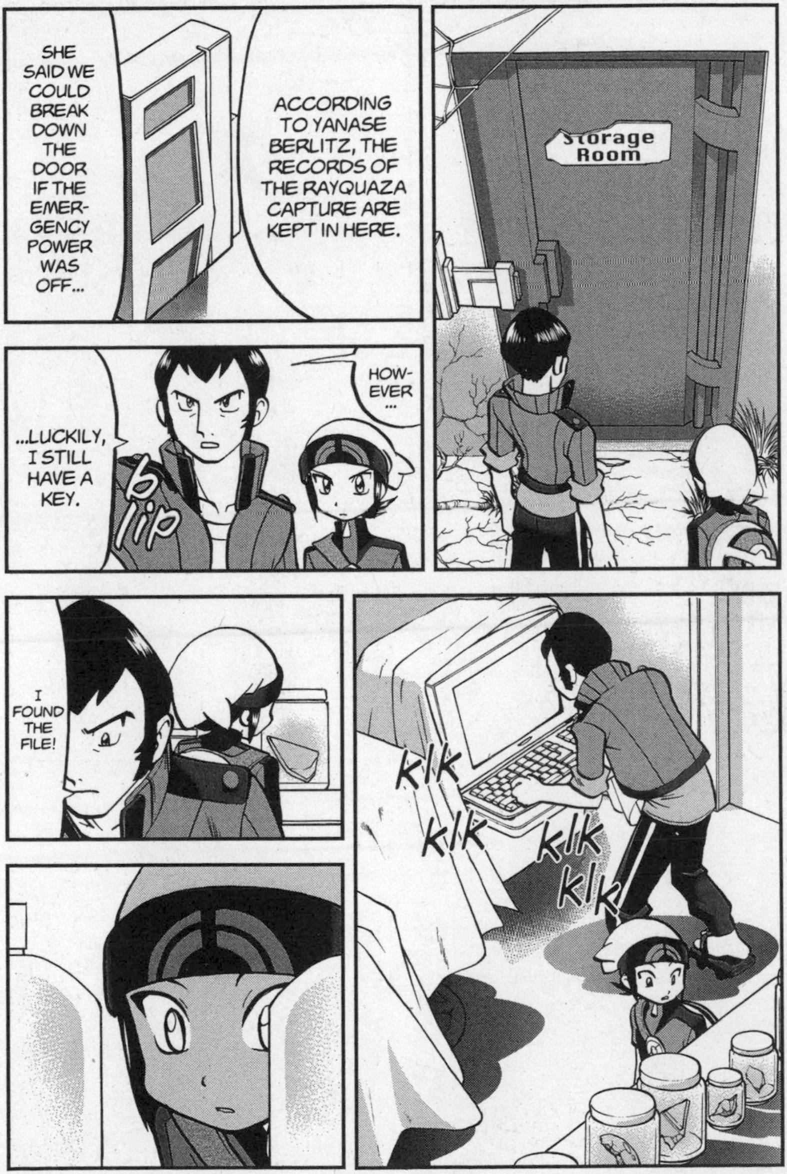
Storage Room
ACCORDING TO YANASE BERLITZ, THE RECORDS OF THE RAYQUAZA CAPTURE ARE KEPT IN HERE.
SHE SAID WE COULD BREAK DOWN THE DOOR IF THE EMER-GENCY POWER WAS OFF...
HOW-EVER ...
...LUCKILY, I STILL HAVE A KEY.
blip
KIK KIK KIK KIK
I FOUND THE FILE!

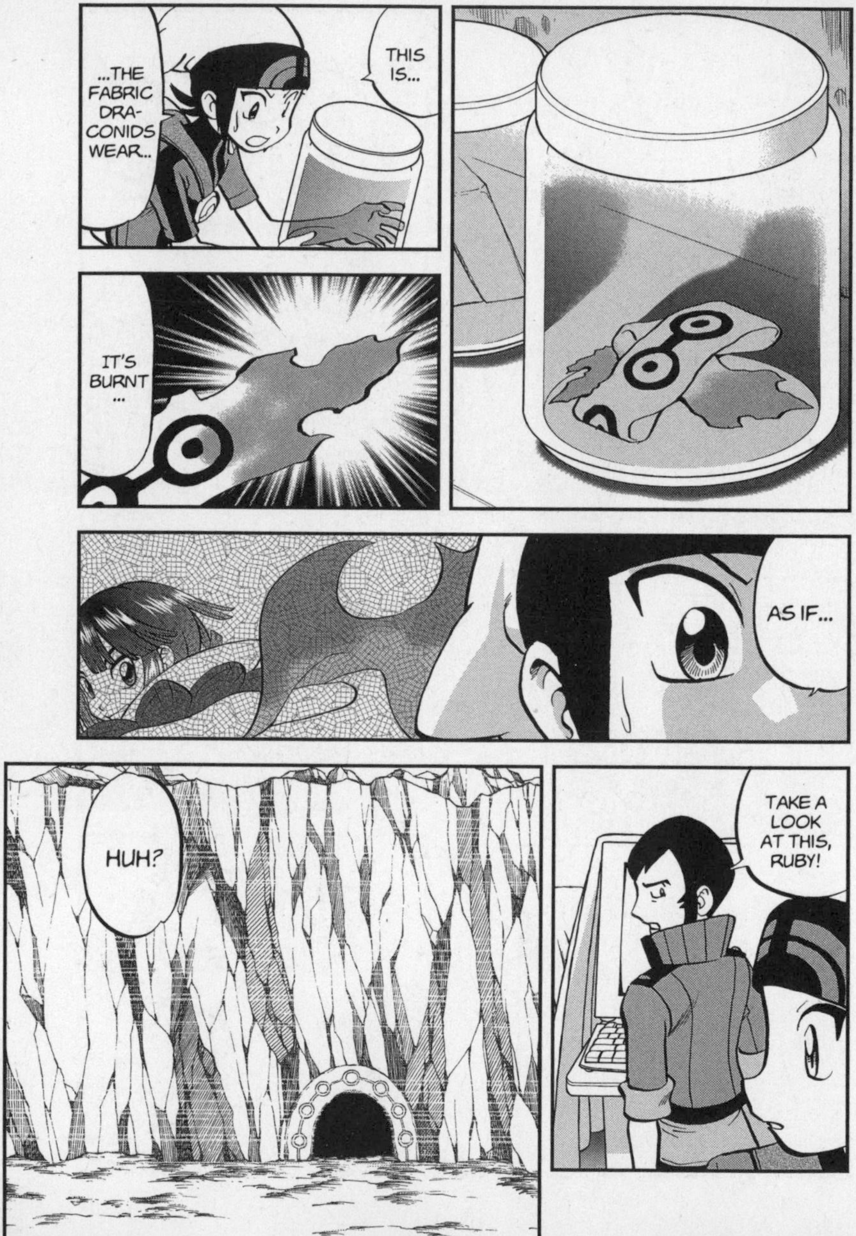
THIS IS...
...THE FABRIC DRA-CONIDS WEAR..
IT'S BURNT ...
AS IF...
TAKE A LOOK AT THIS, RUBY!
HUH?

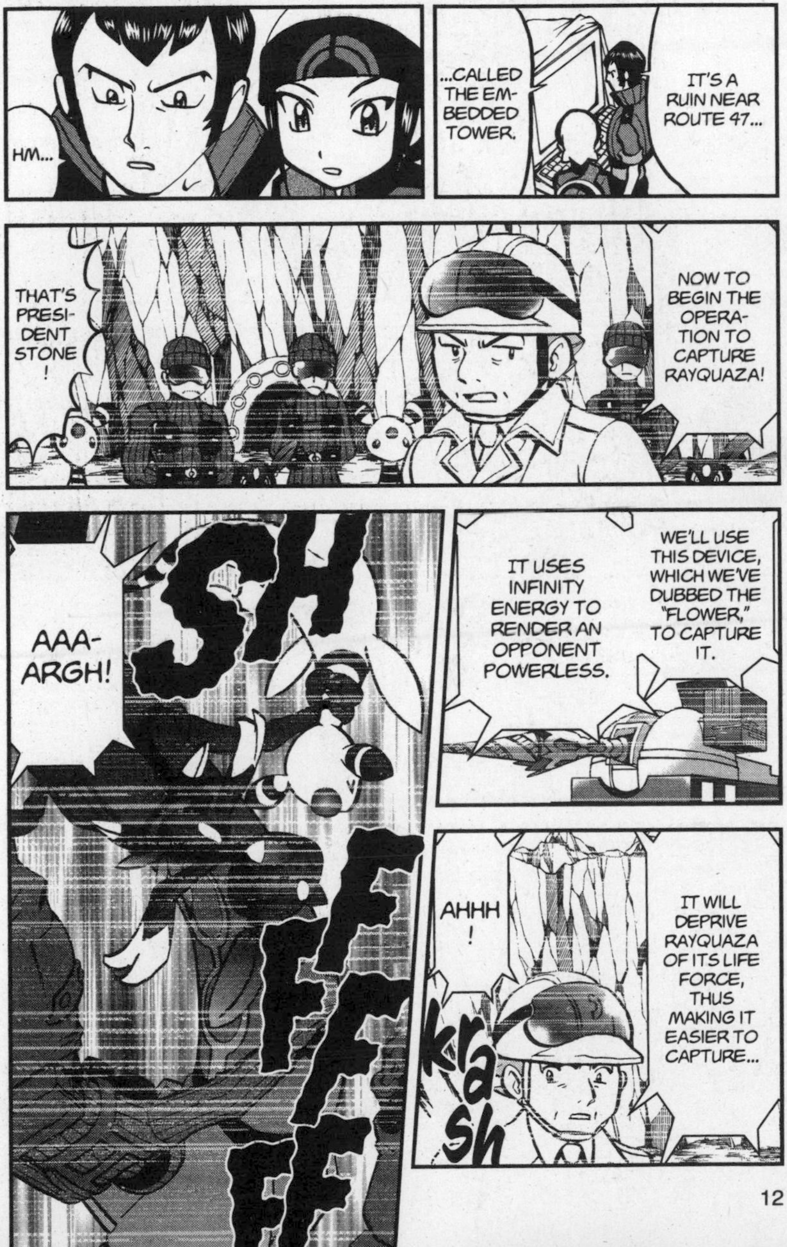
IT'S A RUIN NEAR ROUTE 47...
...CALLED THE EM-BEDDED TOWER.
HM...
NOW TO BEGIN THE OPERA-TION TO CAPTURE RAYQUAZA!
THAT'S PRESI-DENT STONE!
WE'LL USE THIS DEVICE, WHICH WE'VE DUBBED THE "FLOWER," TO CAPTURE IT.
IT USES INFINITY ENERGY TO RENDER AN OPPONENT POWERLESS.
IT WILL DEPRIVE RAYQUAZA OF ITS LIFE FORCE, THUS MAKING IT EASIER TO CAPTURE...
AHHH!
krash
AAA-ARGH!
SHFFFF

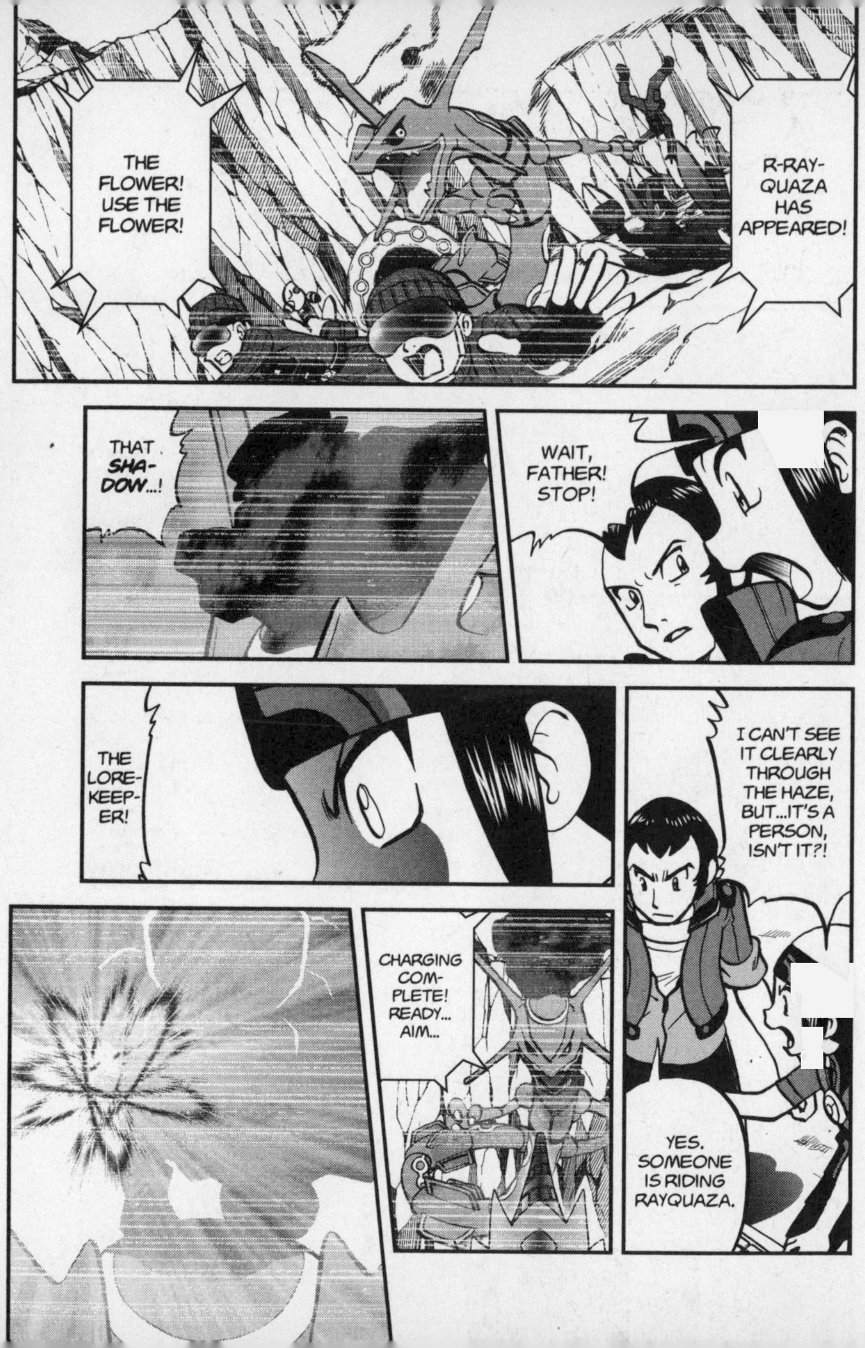
R-RAYQUAZA HAS APPEARED!
THE FLOWER! USE THE FLOWER!
WAIT, FATHER! STOP!
THAT SHADOW...!
I CAN'T SEE IT CLEARLY THROUGH THE HAZE, BUT...IT'S A PERSON, ISN'T IT?!
YES. SOMEONE IS RIDING RAYQUAZA.
THE LOREKEEPER!
CHARGING COMPLETE! READY... AIM...

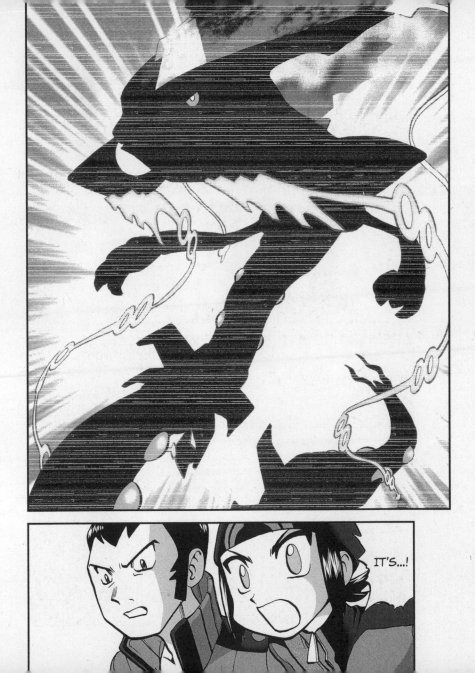

IT'S...!

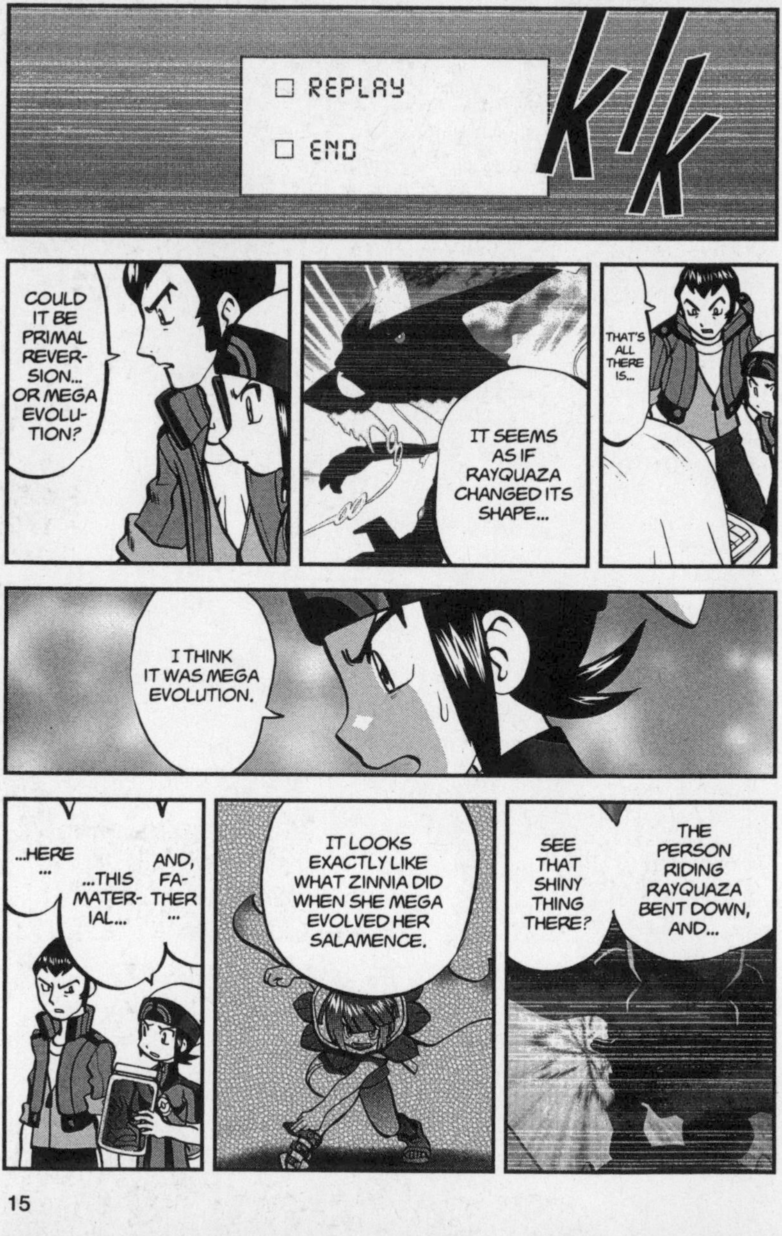

REPLAY
END
K'K
THAT'S ALL THERE IS...
IT SEEMS AS IF RAYQUAZA CHANGED ITS SHAPE...
COULD IT BE PRIMAL REVERSION... OR MEGA EVOLUTION?
I THINK IT WAS MEGA EVOLUTION.
THE PERSON RIDING RAYQUAZA BENT DOWN, AND...
SEE THAT SHINY THING THERE?
IT LOOKS EXACTLY LIKE WHAT ZINNIA DID WHEN SHE MEGA EVOLVED HER SALAMENCE.
AND, FATHER...
...THIS MATERIAL...
...HERE...

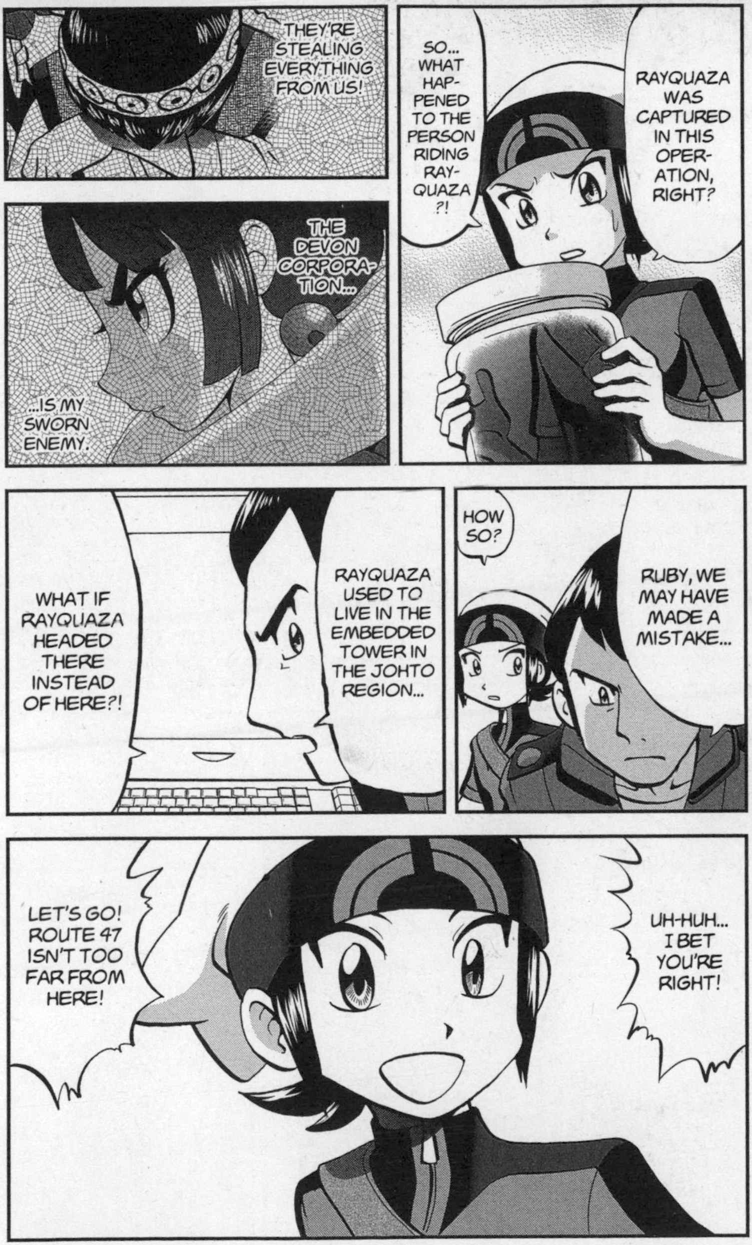
RAYQUAZA WAS CAPTURED IN THIS OPERATION, RIGHT?
SO... WHAT HAPPENED TO THE PERSON RIDING RAYQUAZA?!
THEY'RE STEALING EVERYTHING FROM US!
THE DEVON CORPORATION...
...IS MY SWORN ENEMY.
RUBY, WE MAY HAVE MADE A MISTAKE...
HOW SO?
RAYQUAZA USED TO LIVE IN THE EMBEDDED TOWER IN THE JOHTO REGION...
WHAT IF RAYQUAZA HEADED THERE INSTEAD OF HERE?!
UH-HUH... I BET YOU'RE RIGHT!
LET'S GO! ROUTE 47 ISN'T TOO FAR FROM HERE!

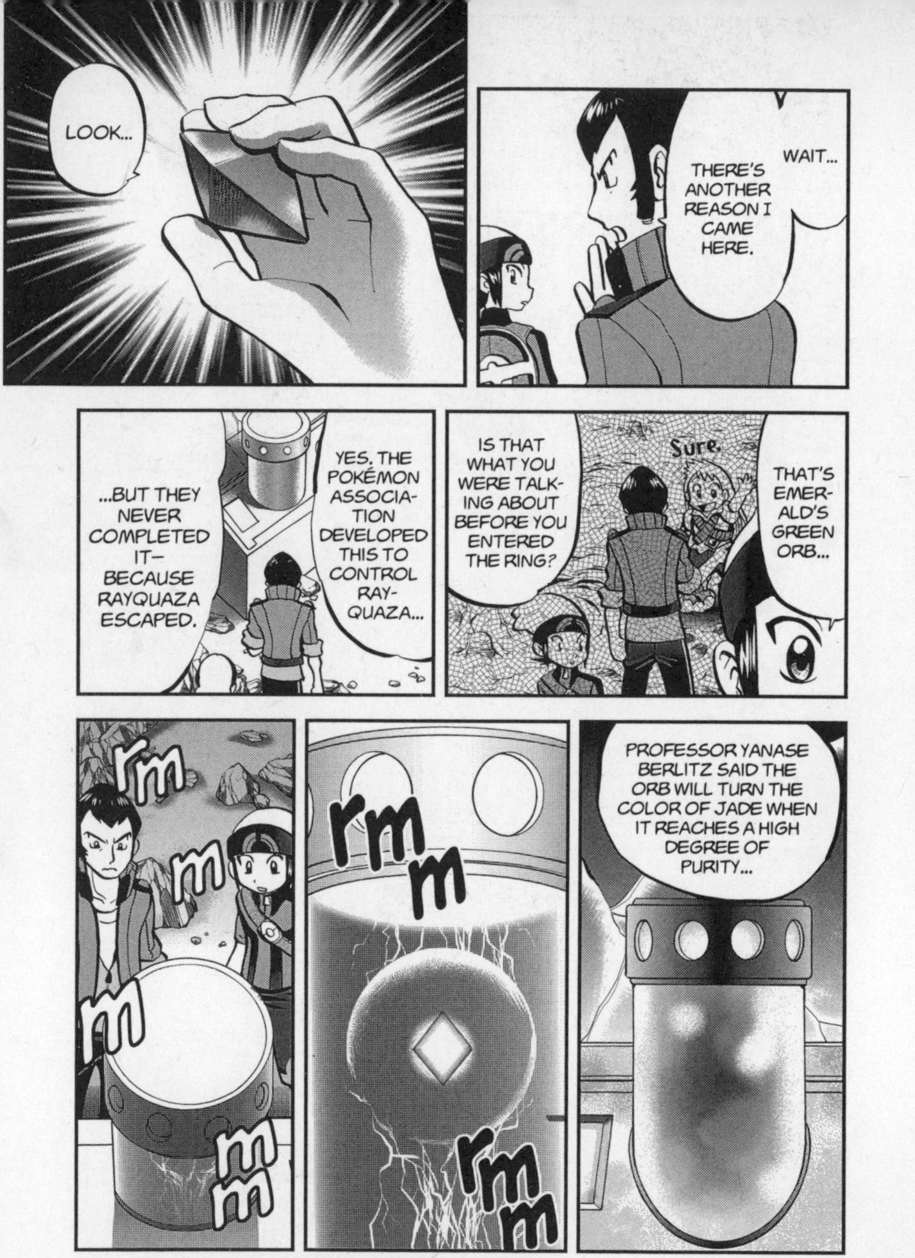
WAIT...
THERE'S ANOTHER REASON I CAME HERE.
LOOK...
THAT'S EMERALD'S GREEN ORB...
Sure.
IS THAT WHAT YOU WERE TALKING ABOUT BEFORE YOU ENTERED THE RING?
YES, THE POKÉMON ASSOCIATION DEVELOPED THIS TO CONTROL RAYQUAZA...
...BUT THEY NEVER COMPLETED IT—BECAUSE RAYQUAZA ESCAPED.
PROFESSOR YANASE BERLITZ SAID THE ORB WILL TURN THE COLOR OF JADE WHEN IT REACHES A HIGH DEGREE OF PURITY...
rm m
rm m
rm m m
m m

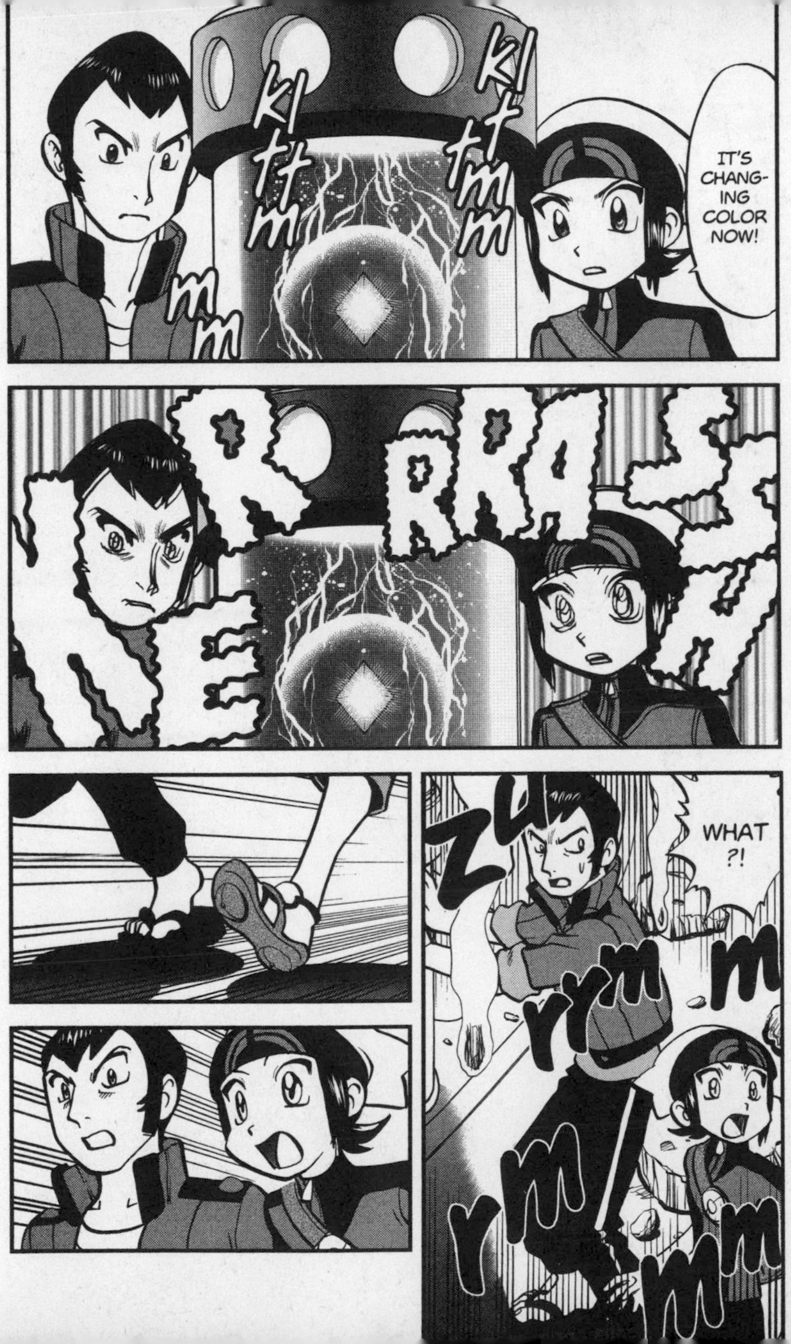

IT'S CHANGING COLOR NOW!
WHAT ?!

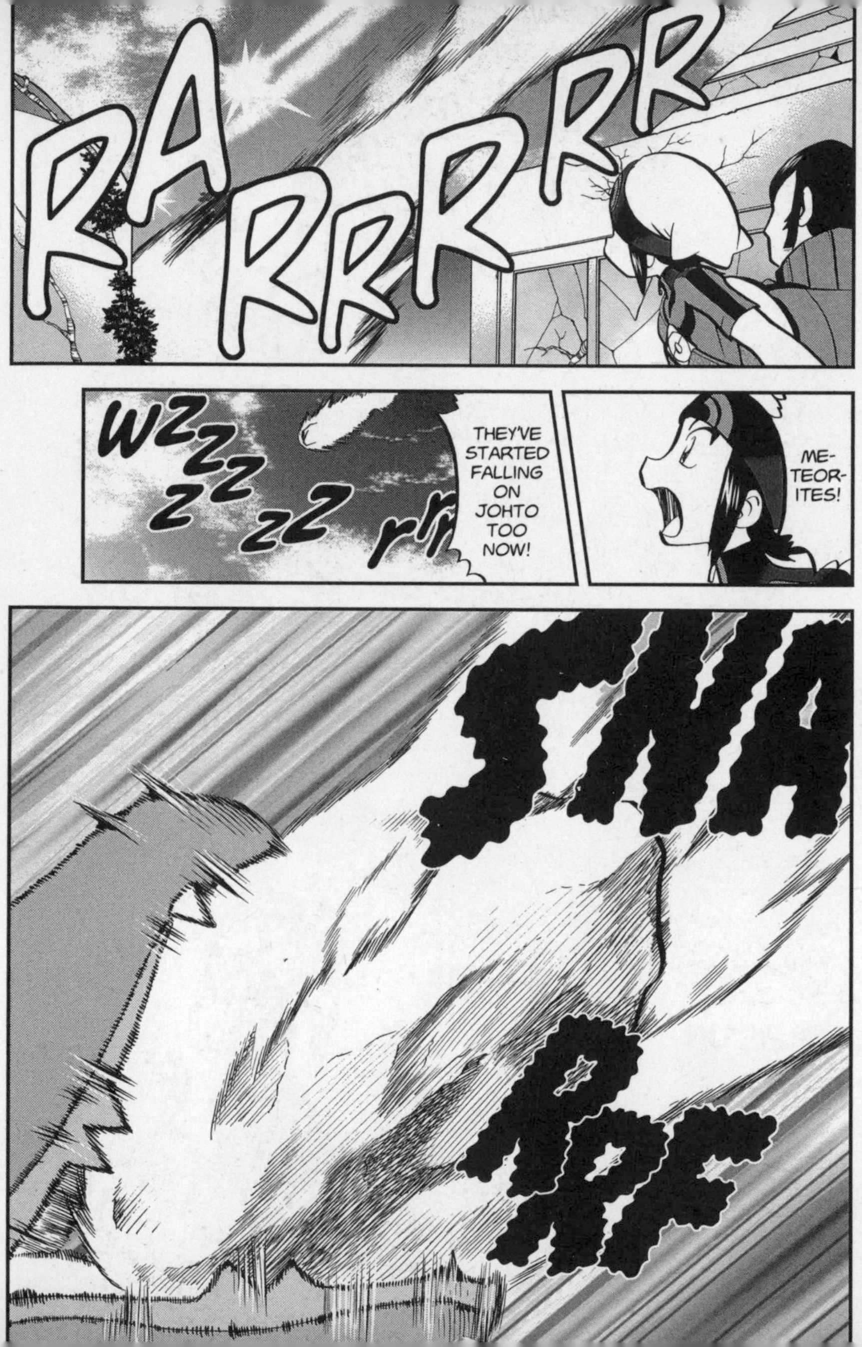
RARRRRRR
ME-TEOR-ITES!
THEY'VE STARTED FALLING ON JOHTO TOO NOW!
WZZZZZZZ rrr
SNARRF

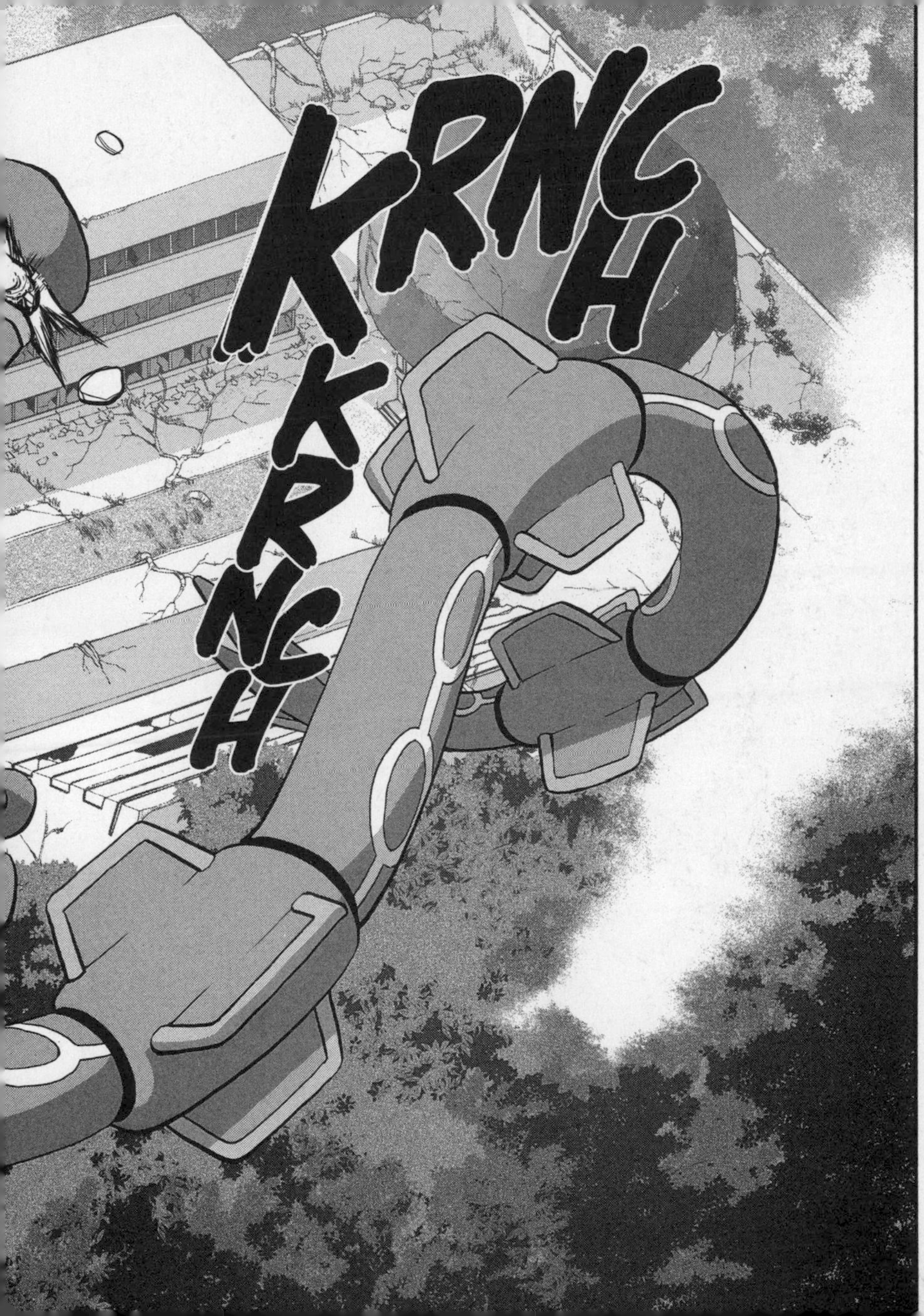
KRNCH
KRNCH

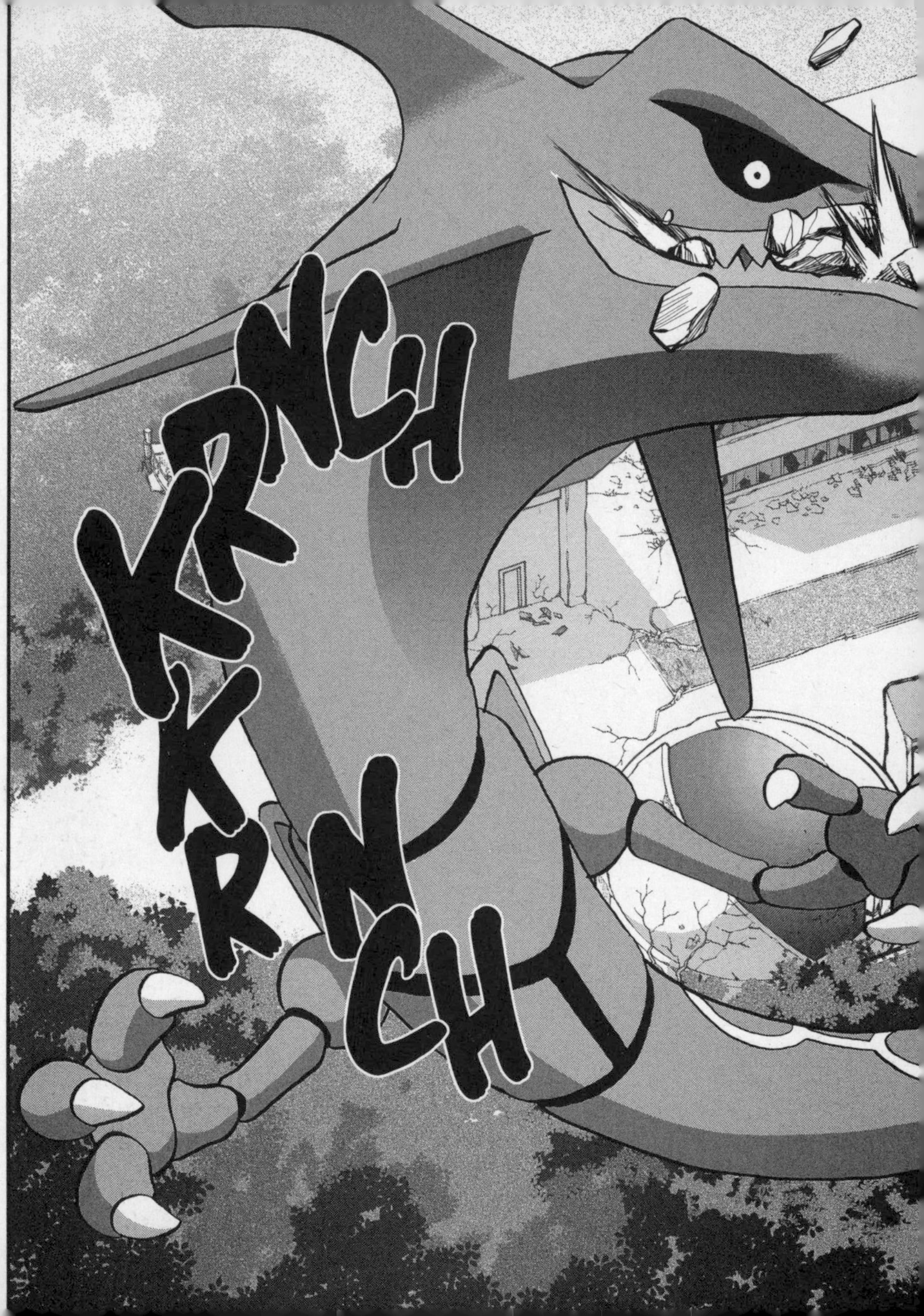
KRNCH
KRNCH

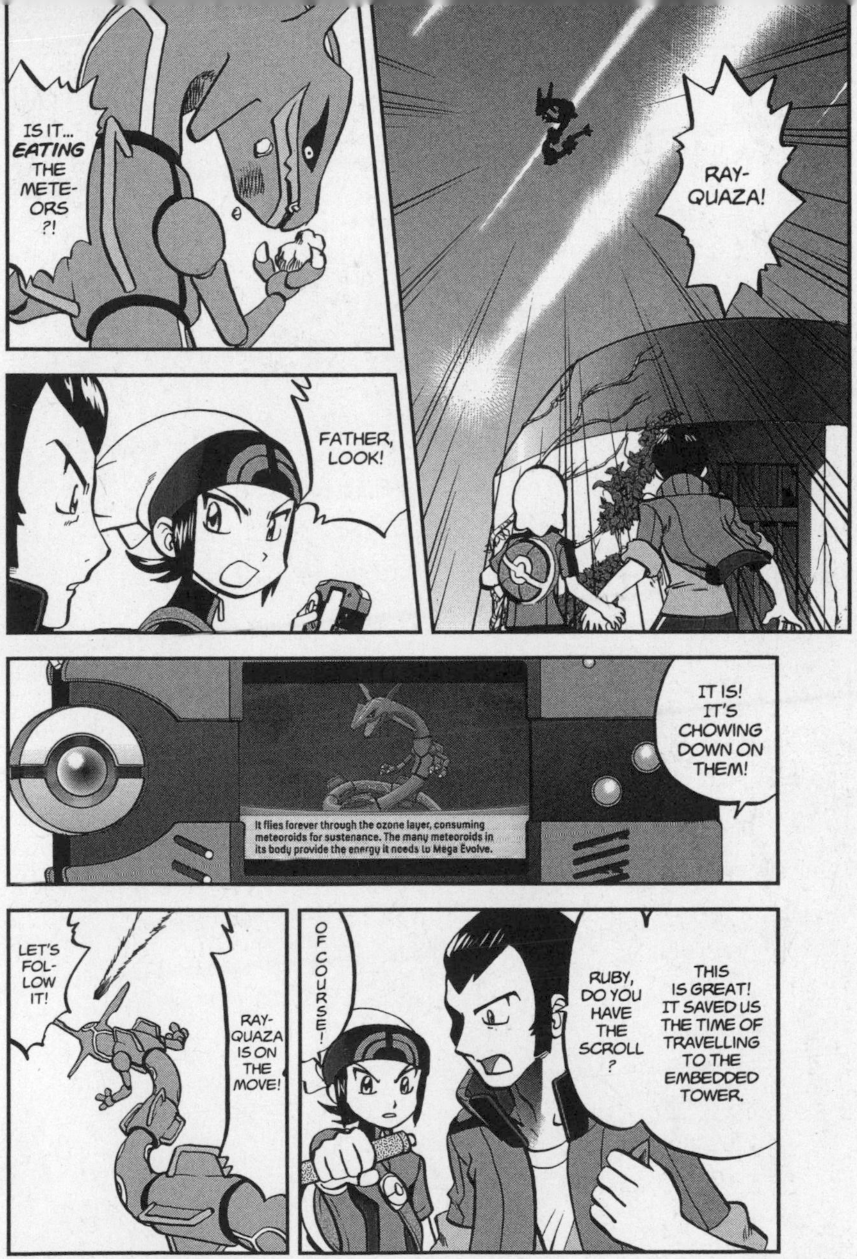
RAY-QUAZA!
IS IT... *EATING* THE METE-ORS?!
FATHER, LOOK!
IT IS! IT'S CHOWING DOWN ON THEM!
It flies forever through the ozone layer, consuming meteoroids for sustenance. The many meteoroids in its body provide the energy it needs to Mega Evolve.
THIS IS GREAT! IT SAVED US THE TIME OF TRAVELLING TO THE EMBEDDED TOWER.
RUBY, DO YOU HAVE THE SCROLL?
OF COURSE!
RAY-QUAZA IS ON THE MOVE!
LET'S FOL-LOW IT!

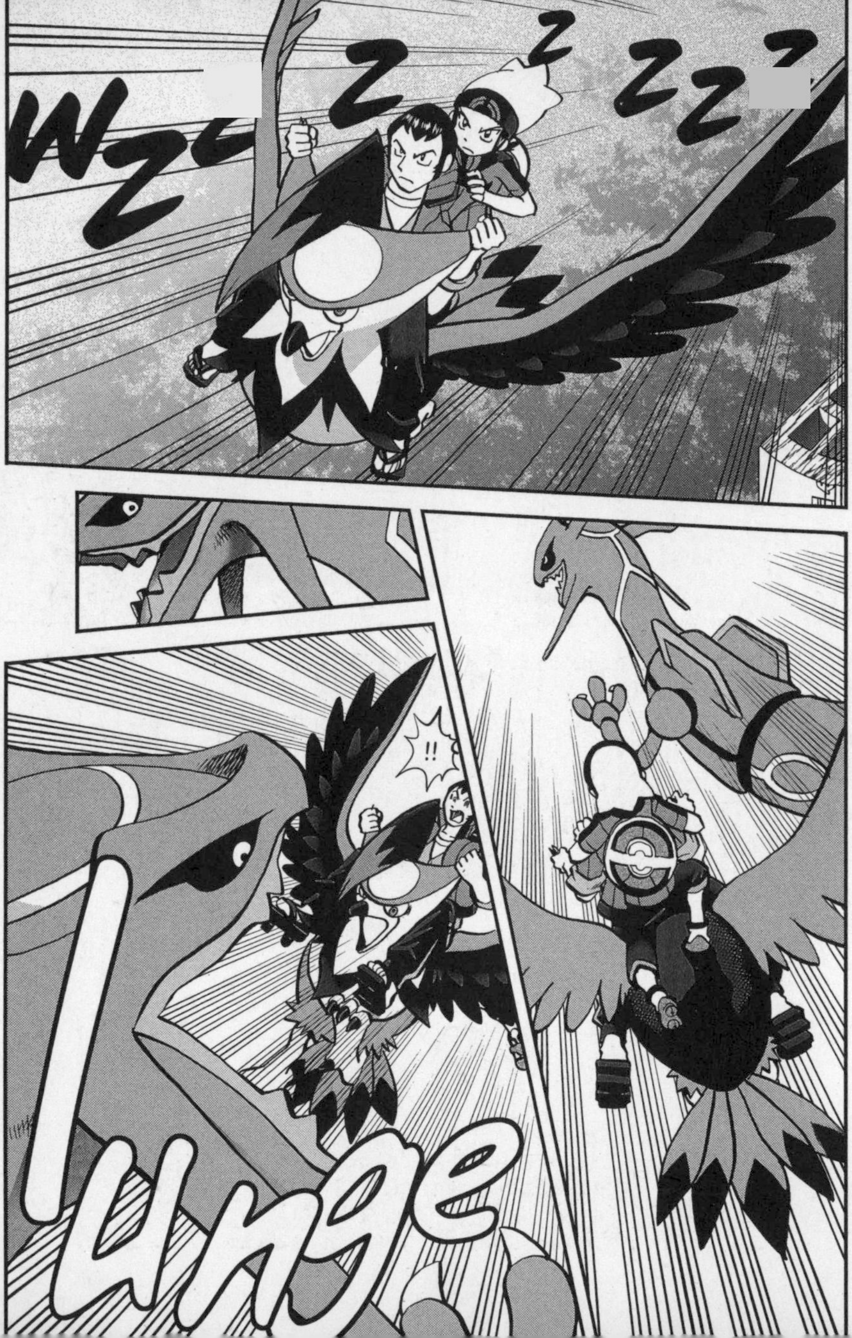
WZZZZZZZ
!!
Lunge

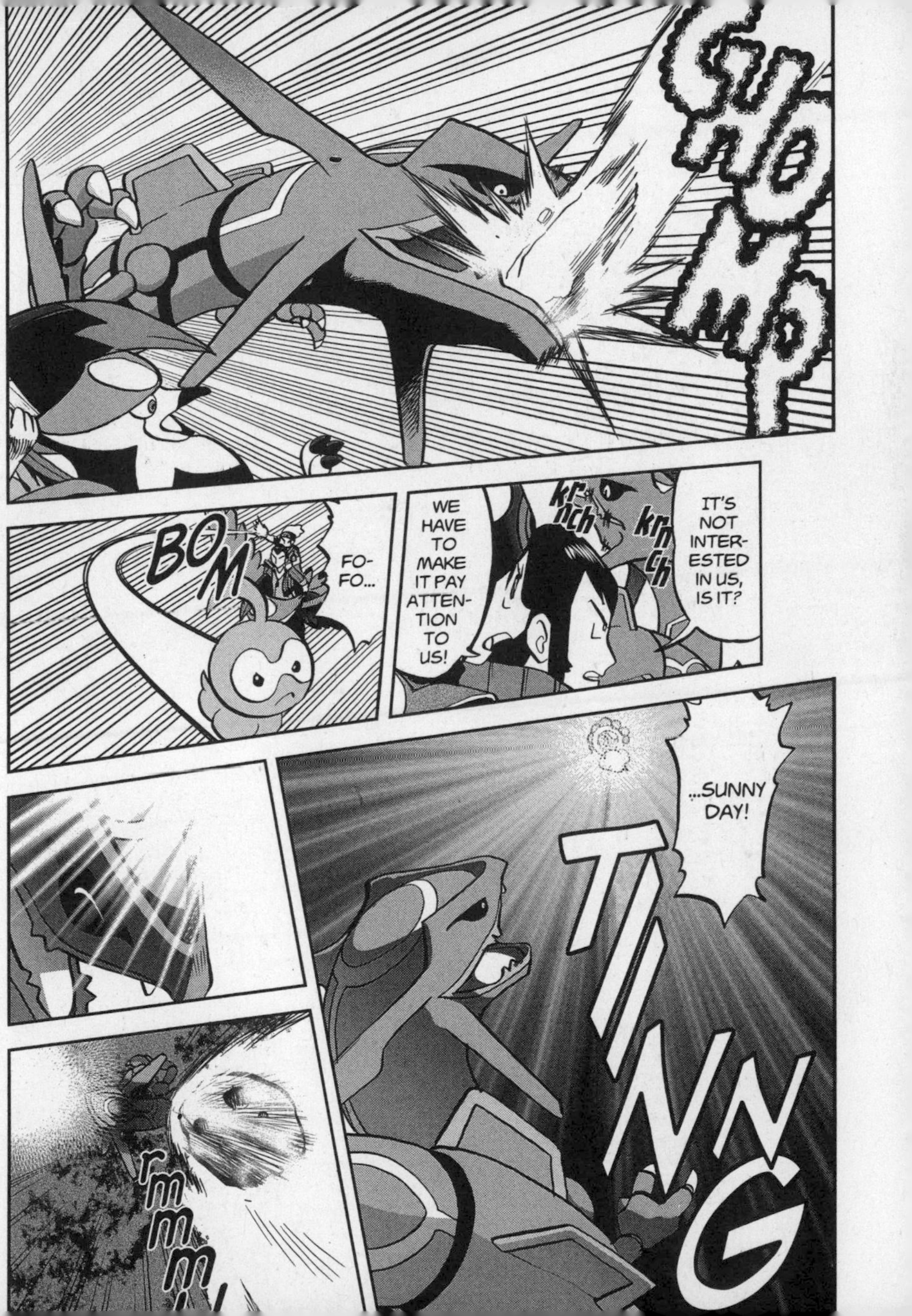
CHOMP
IT'S NOT INTERESTED IN US, IS IT?
krnch krnch
WE HAVE TO MAKE IT PAY ATTENTION TO US!
FO-FO...
BOM
...SUNNY DAY!
TIINNG
rmmm

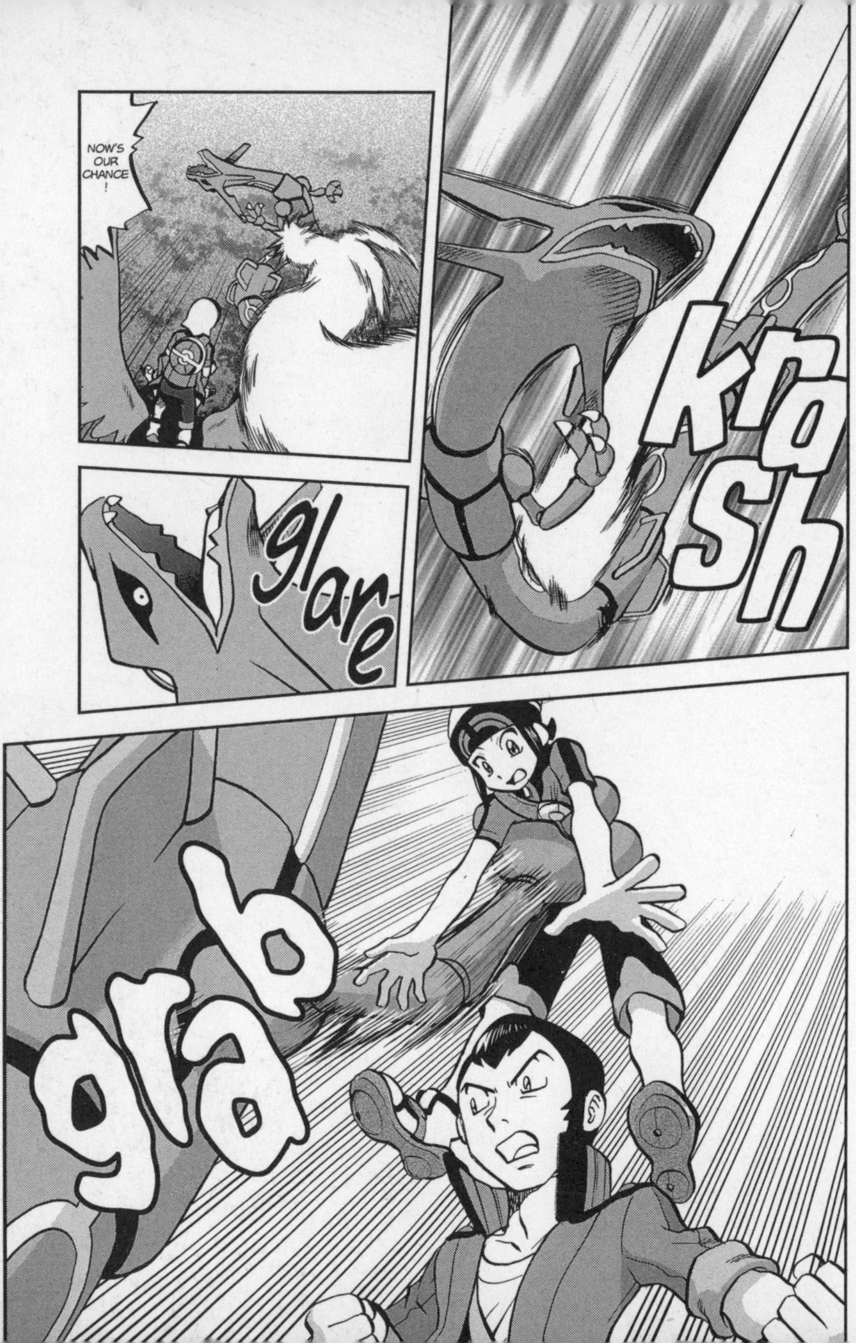
krash
NOW'S OUR CHANCE!
glare
grab

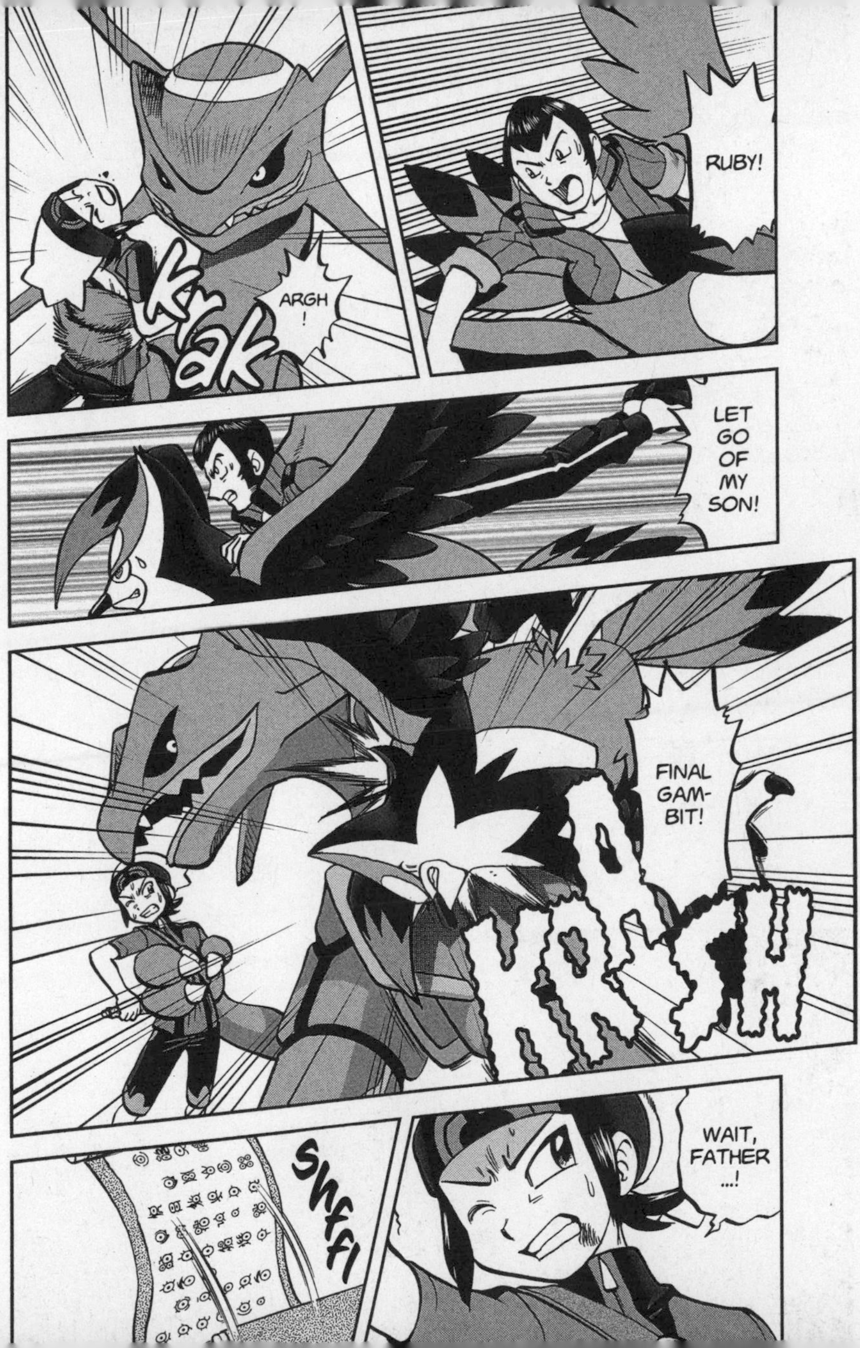

RUBY!
ARGH!
KRAK
LET GO OF MY SON!
FINAL GAMBIT!
KRASH
WAIT, FATHER...!
SWFF!

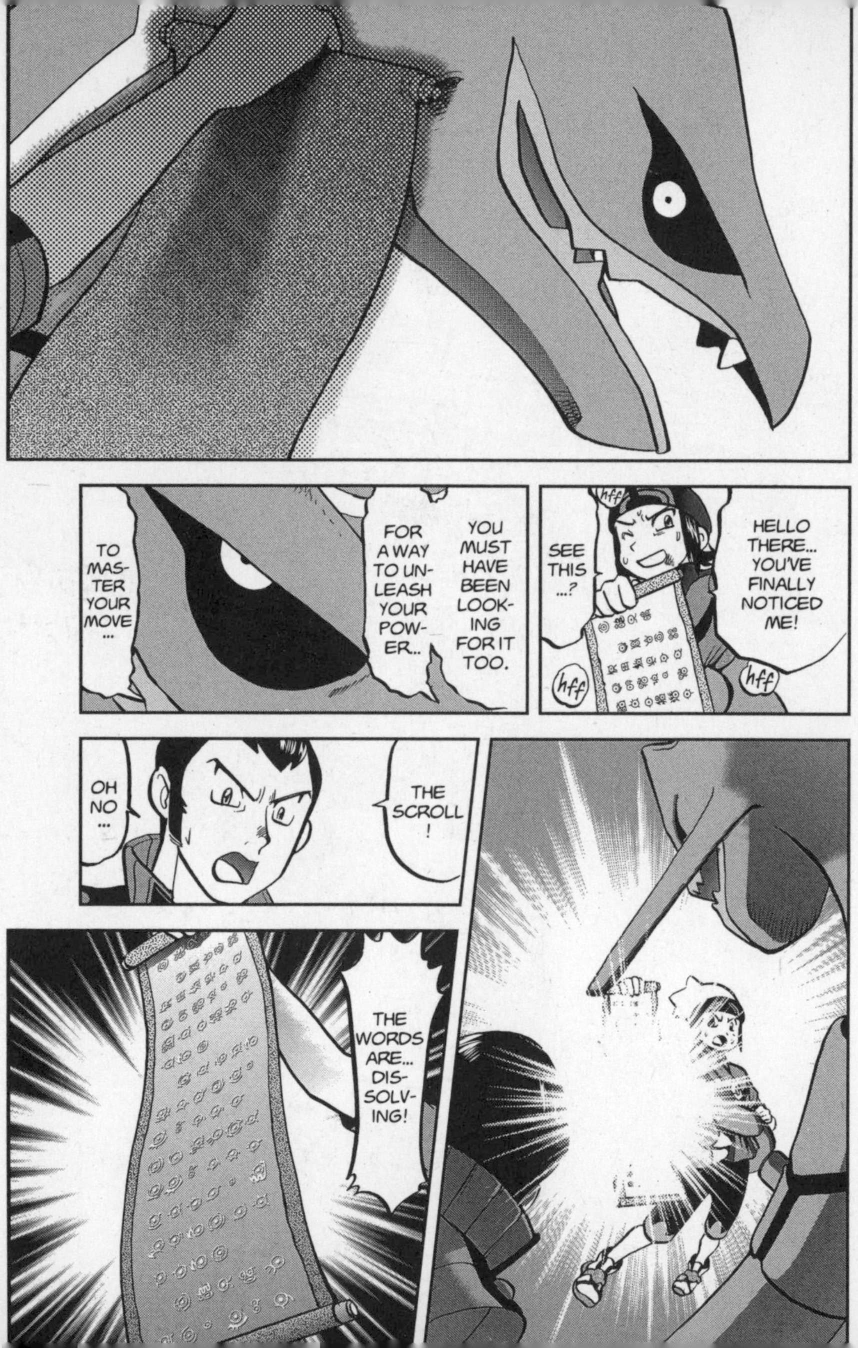
HELLO THERE... YOU'VE FINALLY NOTICED ME!
SEE THIS ...?
hff
hff
YOU MUST HAVE BEEN LOOKING FOR IT TOO.
FOR A WAY TO UNLEASH YOUR POWER...
TO MASTER YOUR MOVE ...
THE SCROLL!
OH NO ...
THE WORDS ARE... DISSOLVING!

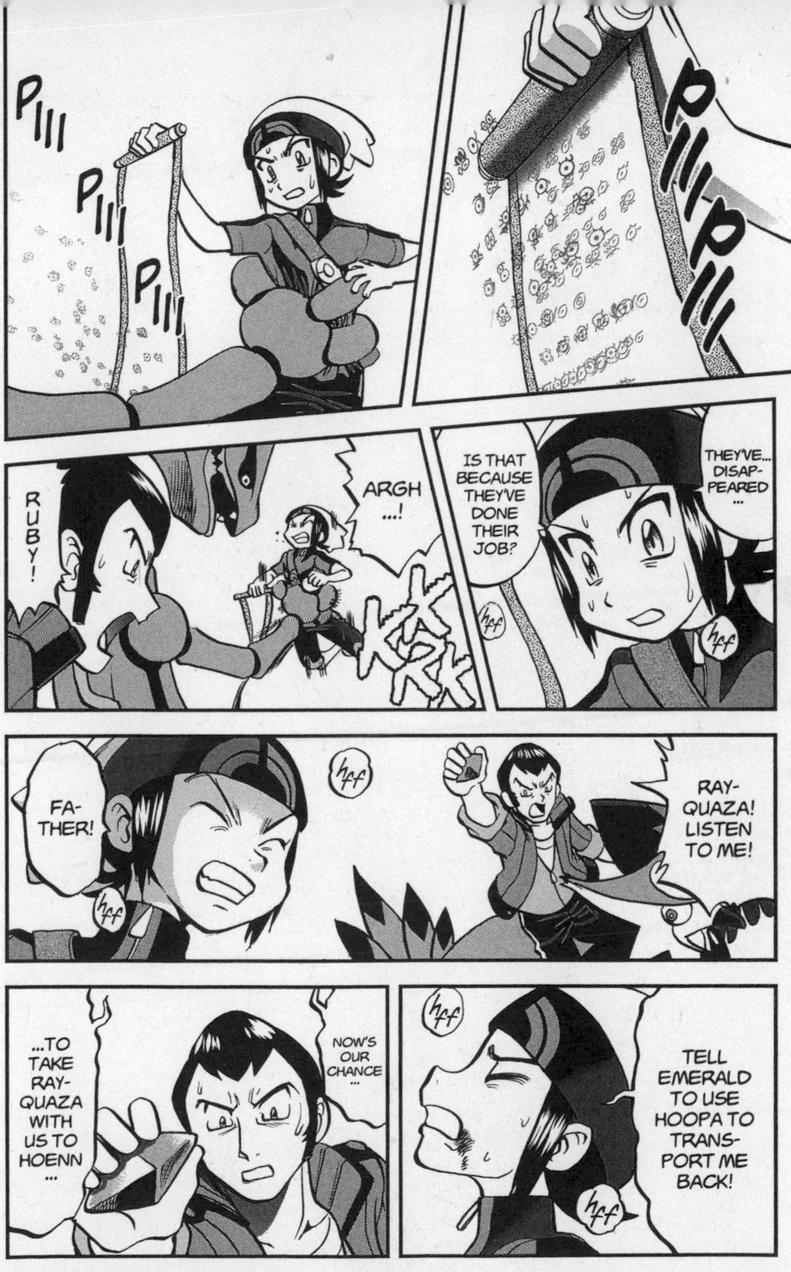
PIIIPIII
PIII PIII PIII
THEY'VE... DISAPPEARED...
IS THAT BECAUSE THEY'VE DONE THEIR JOB?
hff
hff
ARGH ...!
RUBY!
FATHER!
hff
hff
RAYQUAZA! LISTEN TO ME!
hff
TELL EMERALD TO USE HOOPA TO TRANSPORT ME BACK!
hff
NOW'S OUR CHANCE...
...TO TAKE RAYQUAZA WITH US TO HOENN...

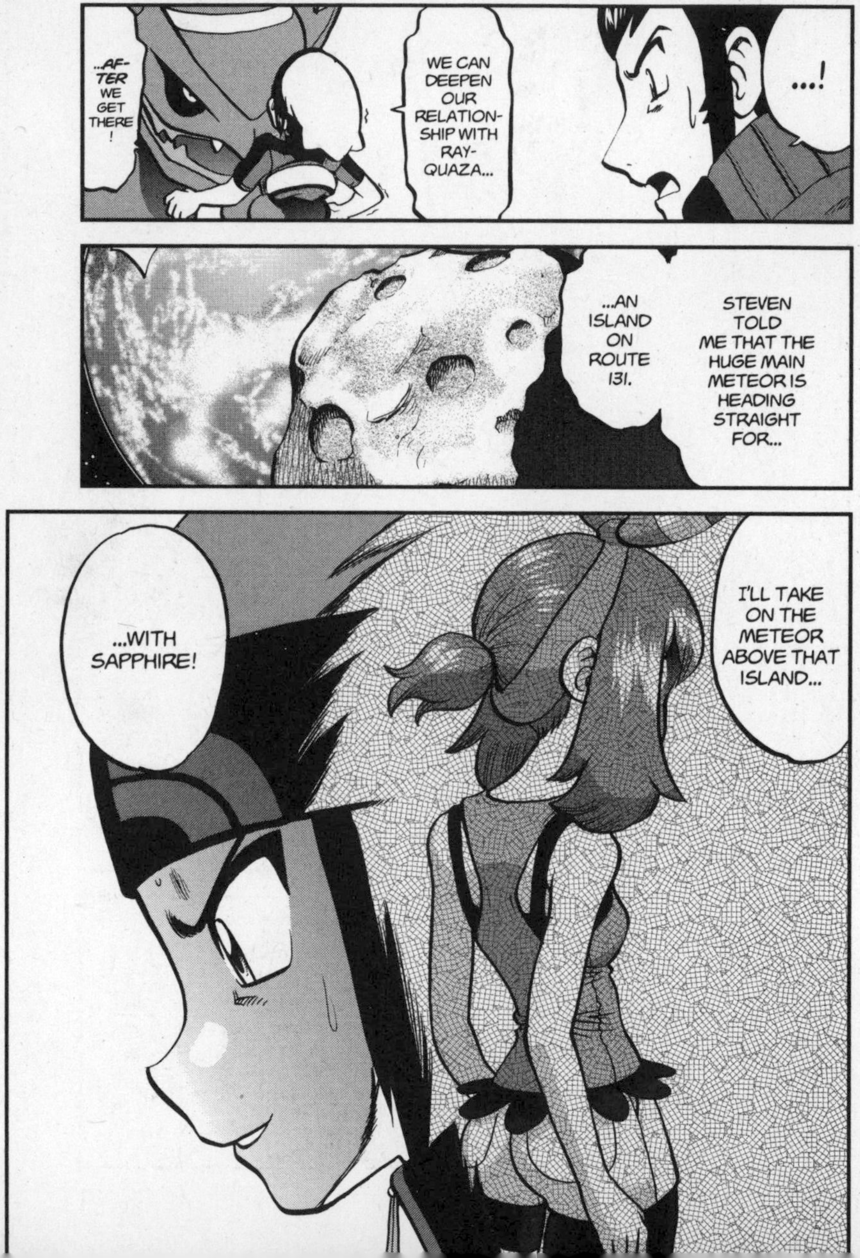
...!
WE CAN DEEPEN OUR RELATIONSHIP WITH RAYQUAZA...
...AFTER WE GET THERE!
STEVEN TOLD ME THAT THE HUGE MAIN METEOR IS HEADING STRAIGHT FOR...
...AN ISLAND ON ROUTE 131.
I'LL TAKE ON THE METEOR ABOVE THAT ISLAND...
...WITH SAPPHIRE!

LABORATORY WING

The place where Rayquaza was captured nine years ago. The capturing of Rayquaza was a top secret project led by the Pokémon Association, and the Devon Corporation was one of the companies that provided technological assistance. The project was brought up as a countermeasure against Groudon and Kyogre but ended in failure.

JOHTO REGION

Many tourists visit this beautiful ancient city.

POKÉMON ASSOCIATION

A public institution that manages the Pokémon League and Gym system. Each region carries out their own League and Gym Leader exams but the Kanto, Johto, Hoenn, and Sinnoh regions all follow the same rules. They are a huge worldwide organization.

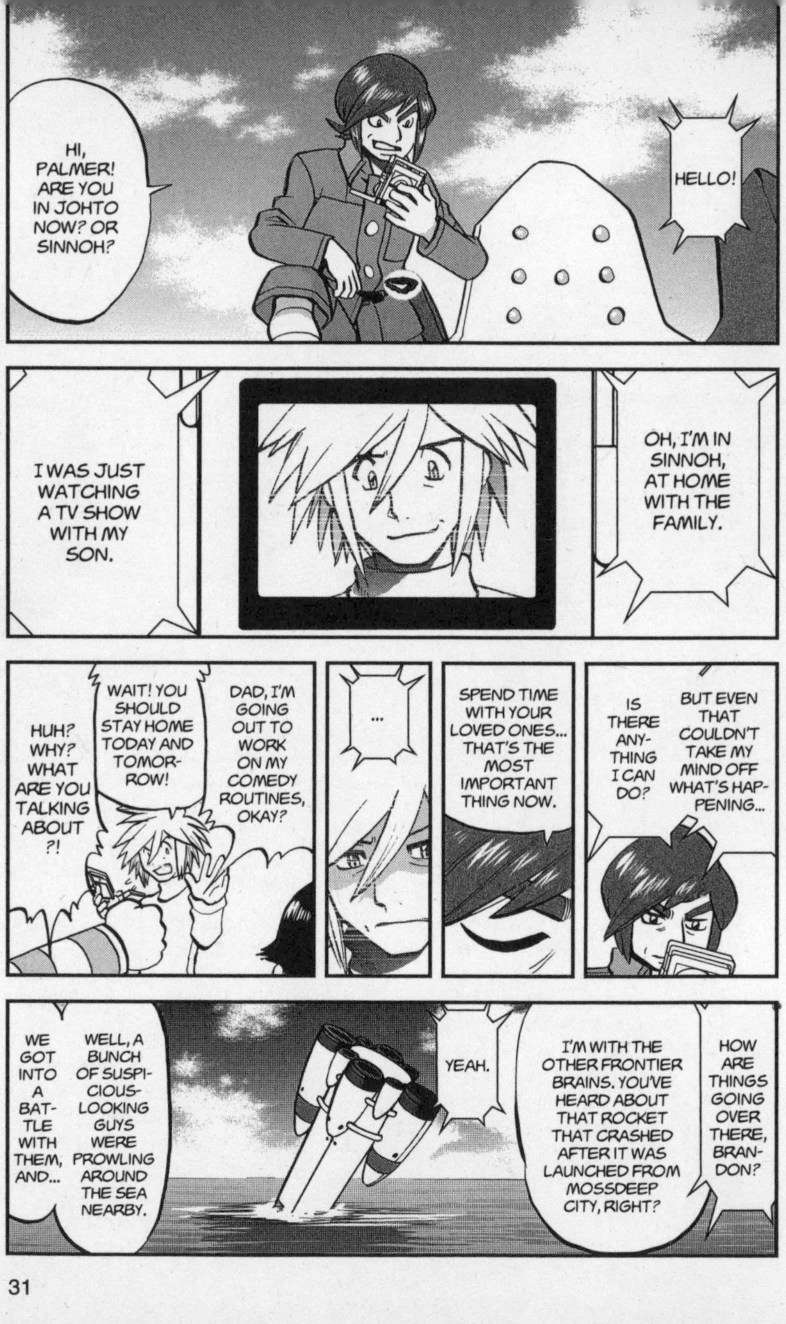
HELLO!
HI, PALMER! ARE YOU IN JOHTO NOW? OR SINNOH?
OH, I'M IN SINNOH, AT HOME WITH THE FAMILY.
I WAS JUST WATCHING A TV SHOW WITH MY SON.
BUT EVEN THAT COULDN'T TAKE MY MIND OFF WHAT'S HAP-PENING...
IS THERE ANY-THING I CAN DO?
SPEND TIME WITH YOUR LOVED ONES... THAT'S THE MOST IMPORTANT THING NOW.
...
DAD, I'M GOING OUT TO WORK ON MY COMEDY ROUTINES, OKAY?
WAIT! YOU SHOULD STAY HOME TODAY AND TOMOR-ROW!
HUH? WHY? WHAT ARE YOU TALKING ABOUT ?!
HOW ARE THINGS GOING OVER THERE, BRAN-DON?
I'M WITH THE OTHER FRONTIER BRAINS. YOU'VE HEARD ABOUT THAT ROCKET THAT CRASHED AFTER IT WAS LAUNCHED FROM MOSSDEEP CITY, RIGHT?
YEAH.
WELL, A BUNCH OF SUSPI-CIOUS-LOOKING GUYS WERE PROWLING AROUND THE SEA NEARBY.
WE GOT INTO A BAT-TLE WITH THEM, AND...

Omega Alpha Adventure 16

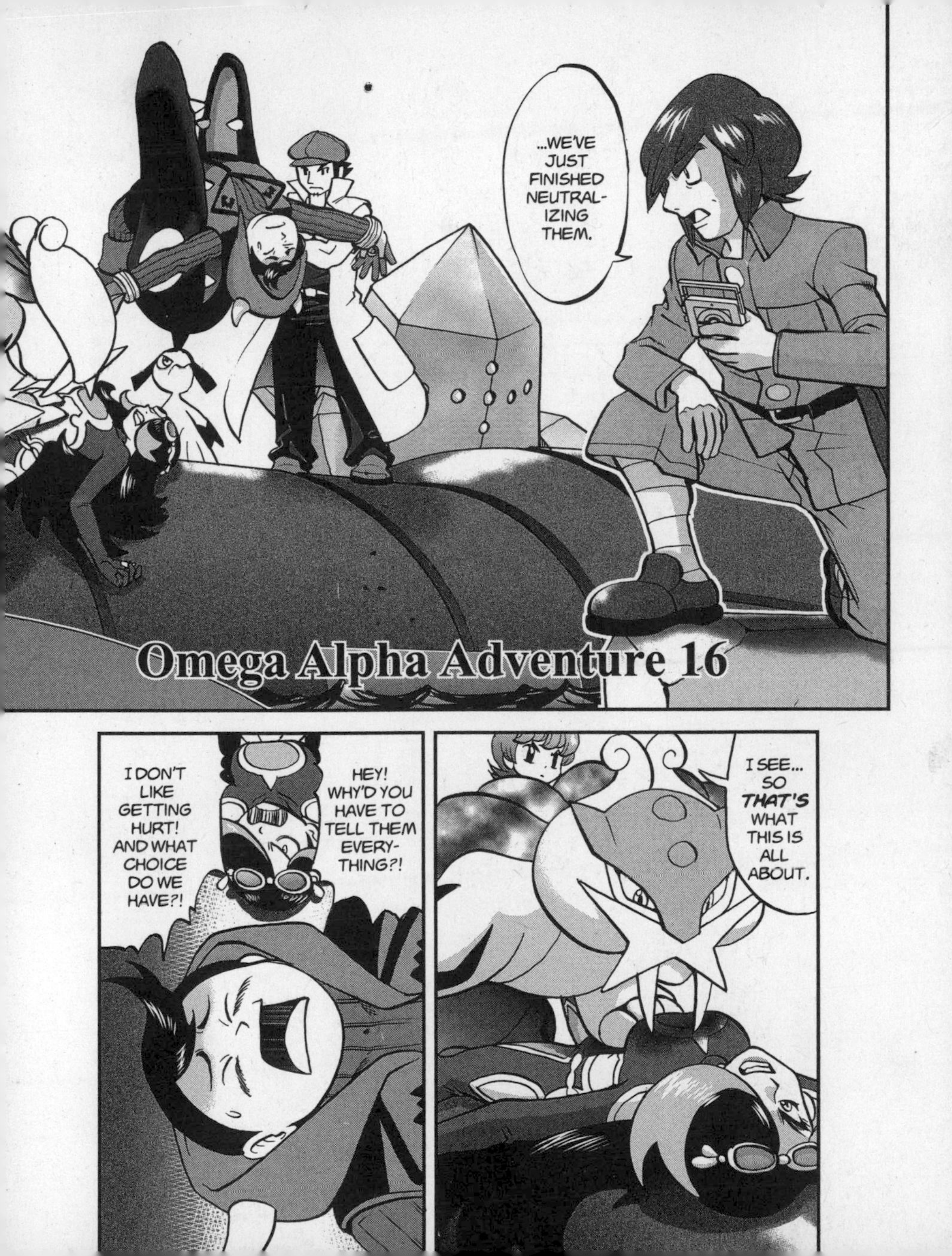
...WE'VE JUST FINISHED NEUTRAL-IZING THEM.
I SEE... SO *THAT'S* WHAT THIS IS ALL ABOUT.
HEY! WHY'D YOU HAVE TO TELL THEM EVERY-THING?!
I DON'T LIKE GETTING HURT! AND WHAT CHOICE DO WE HAVE?!

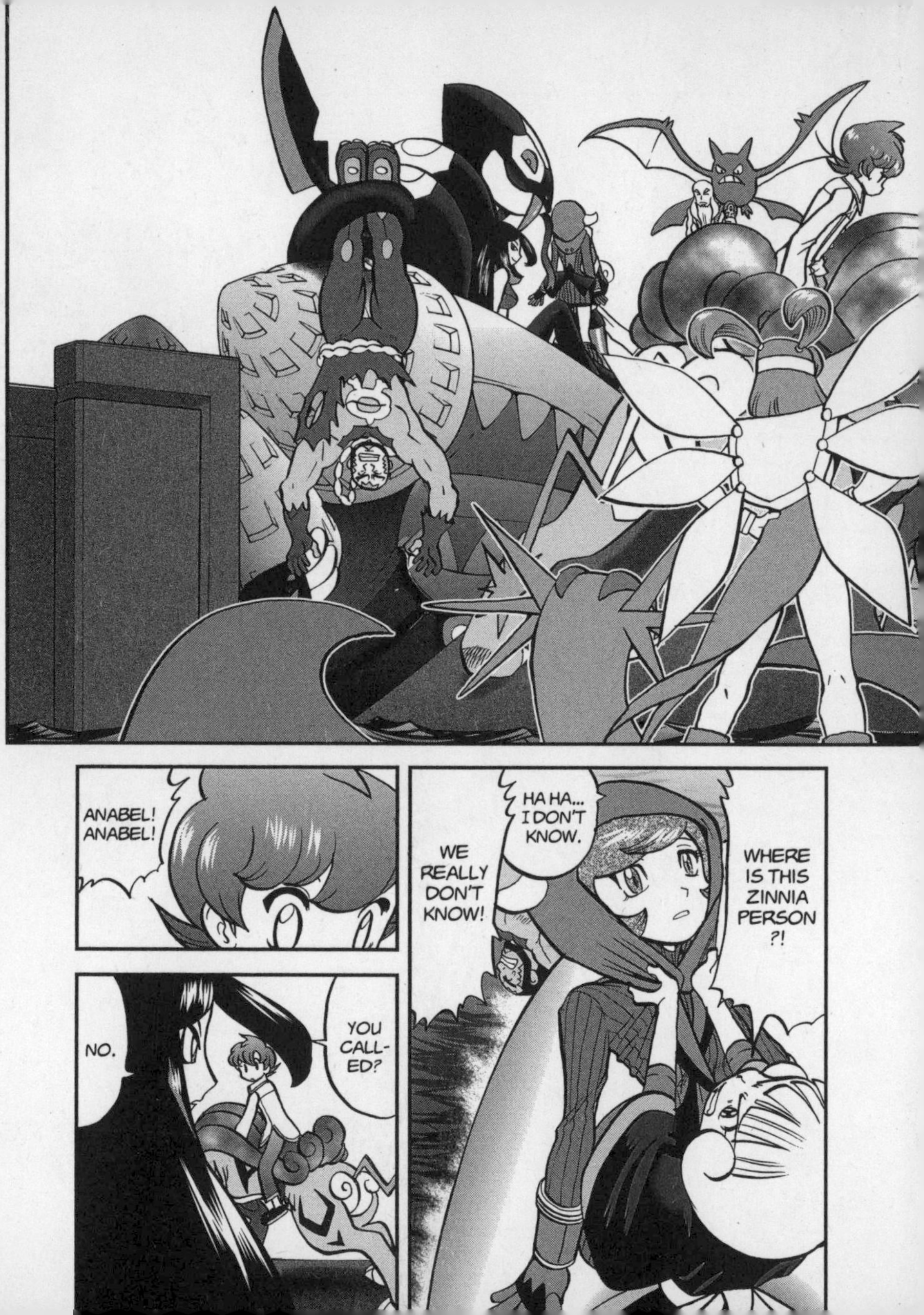
WHERE IS THIS ZINNIA PERSON?!
HA HA... I DON'T KNOW.
WE REALLY DON'T KNOW!
ANABEL! ANABEL!
YOU CALLED-ED?
NO.

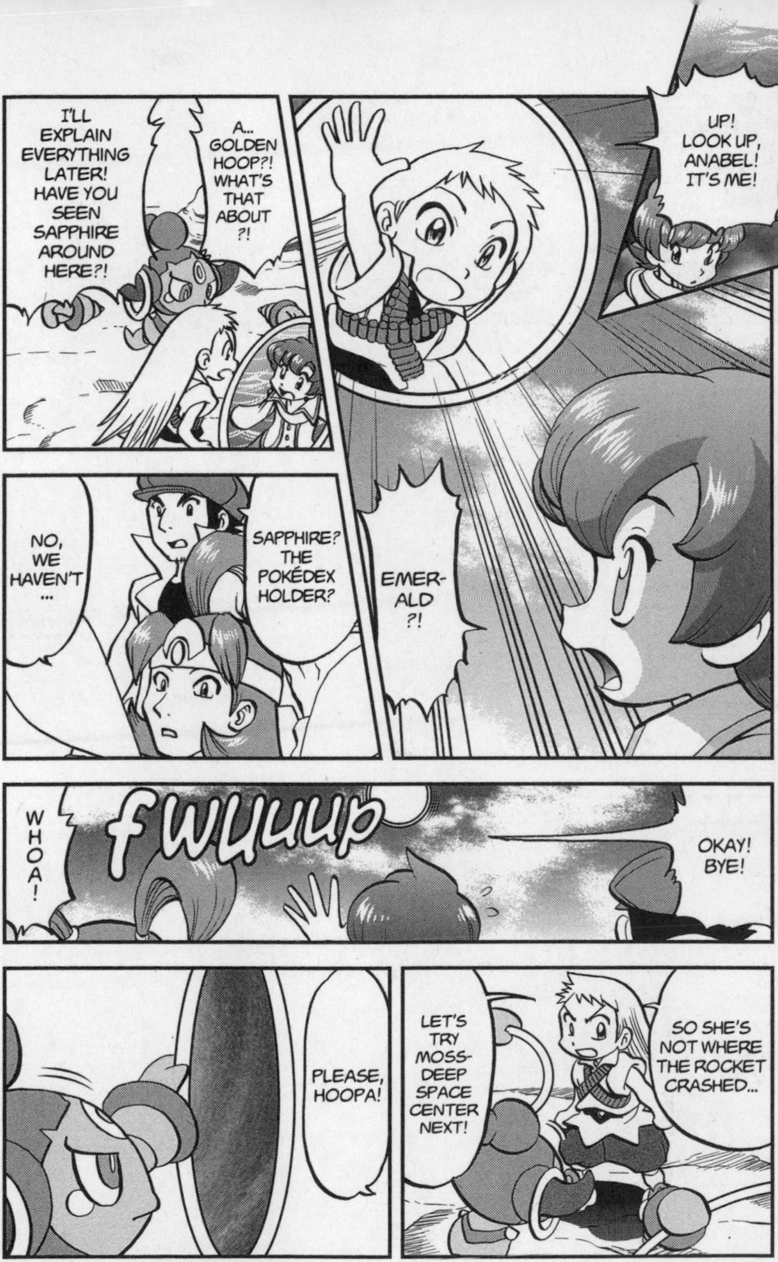
UP! LOOK UP, ANABEL! IT'S ME!
EMER-ALD ?!
A... GOLDEN HOOP?! WHAT'S THAT ABOUT ?!
I'LL EXPLAIN EVERYTHING LATER! HAVE YOU SEEN SAPPHIRE AROUND HERE?!
SAPPHIRE? THE POKÉDEX HOLDER?
NO, WE HAVEN'T ...
OKAY! BYE!
fwuuup
WHOA!
SO SHE'S NOT WHERE THE ROCKET CRASHED...
LET'S TRY MOSS-DEEP SPACE CENTER NEXT!
PLEASE, HOOPA!

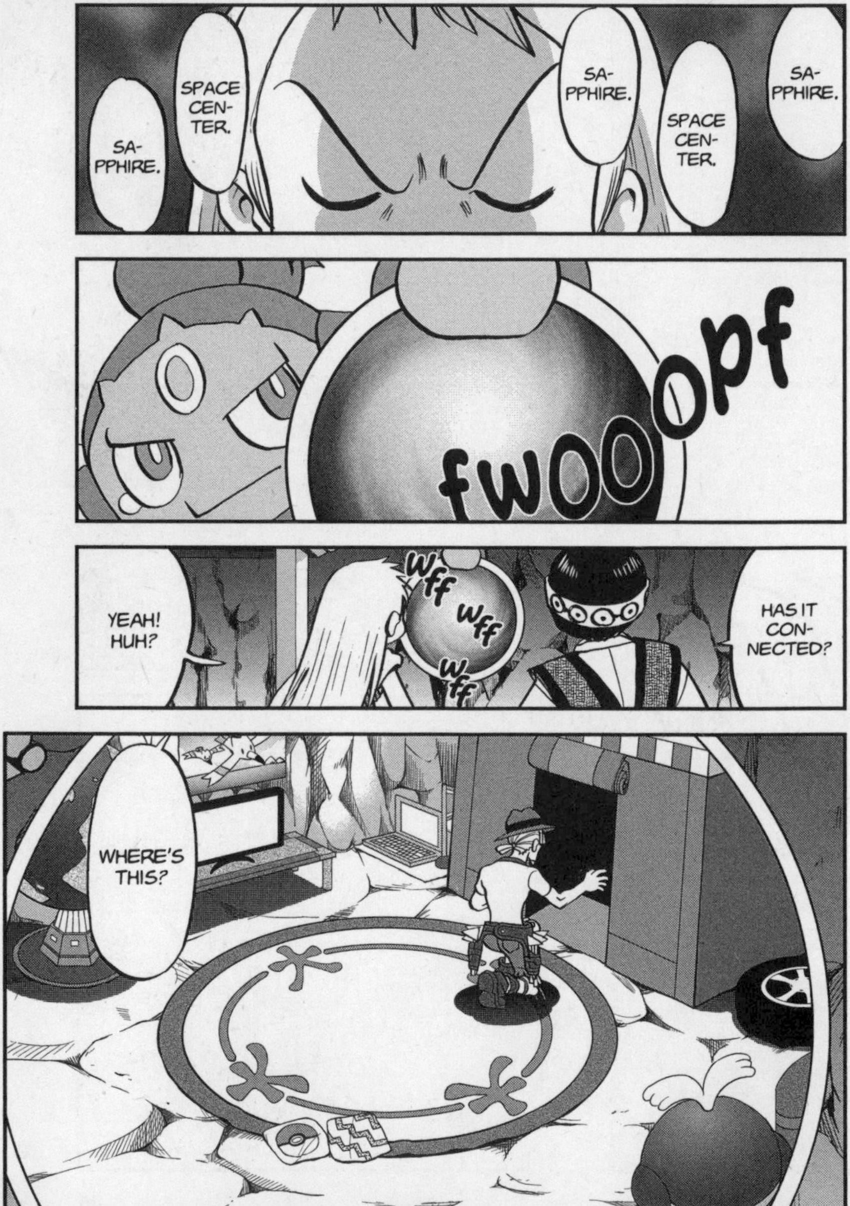
SA-PPHIRE.
SPACE CEN-TER.
SA-PPHIRE.
SPACE CEN-TER.
SA-PPHIRE.
FWOOOPF
HAS IT CON-NECTED?
WFF WFF WFF
YEAH! HUH?
WHERE'S THIS?

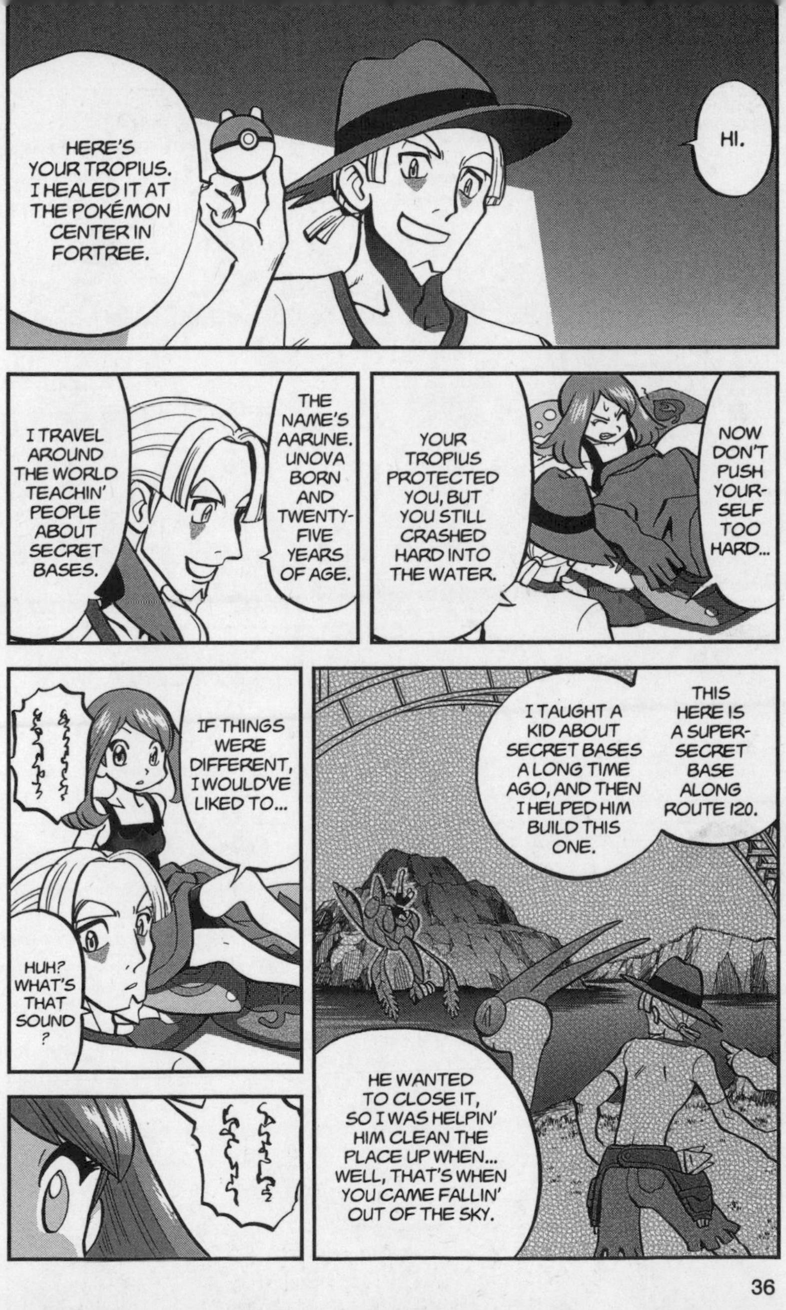
HI.
HERE'S YOUR TROPIUS. I HEALED IT AT THE POKÉMON CENTER IN FORTREE.
NOW DON'T PUSH YOURSELF TOO HARD...
YOUR TROPIUS PROTECTED YOU, BUT YOU STILL CRASHED HARD INTO THE WATER.
THE NAME'S AARUNE. UNOVA BORN AND TWENTY-FIVE YEARS OF AGE.
I TRAVEL AROUND THE WORLD TEACHIN' PEOPLE ABOUT SECRET BASES.
THIS HERE IS A SUPER-SECRET BASE ALONG ROUTE 120.
I TAUGHT A KID ABOUT SECRET BASES A LONG TIME AGO, AND THEN I HELPED HIM BUILD THIS ONE.
HE WANTED TO CLOSE IT, SO I WAS HELPIN' HIM CLEAN THE PLACE UP WHEN... WELL, THAT'S WHEN YOU CAME FALLIN' OUT OF THE SKY.
IF THINGS WERE DIFFERENT, I WOULD'VE LIKED TO...
HUH? WHAT'S THAT SOUND?

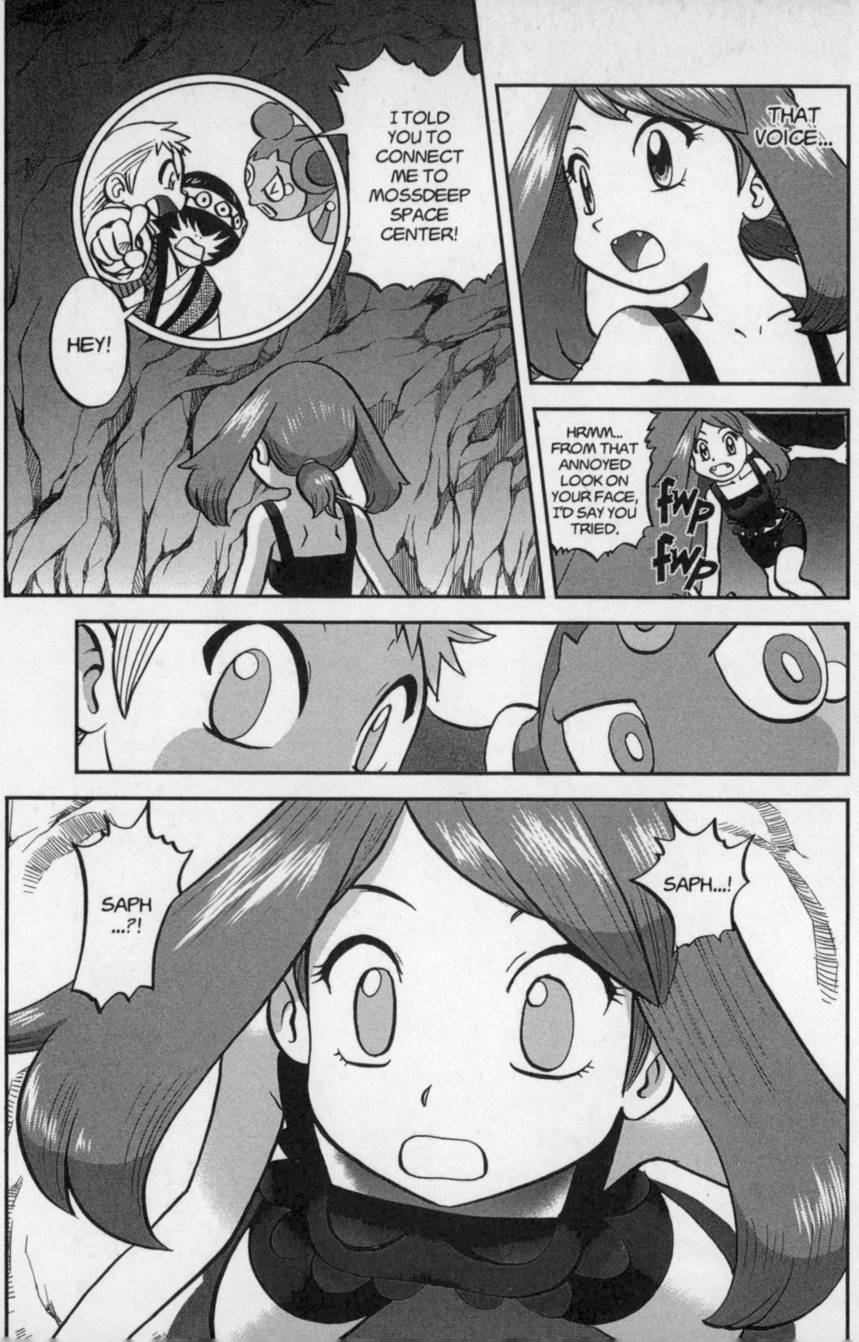
THAT VOICE...
HRMM... FROM THAT ANNOYED LOOK ON YOUR FACE, I'D SAY YOU TRIED.
fwp fwp
I TOLD YOU TO CONNECT ME TO MOSSDEEP SPACE CENTER!
HEY!
SAPH...!
SAPH ...?!

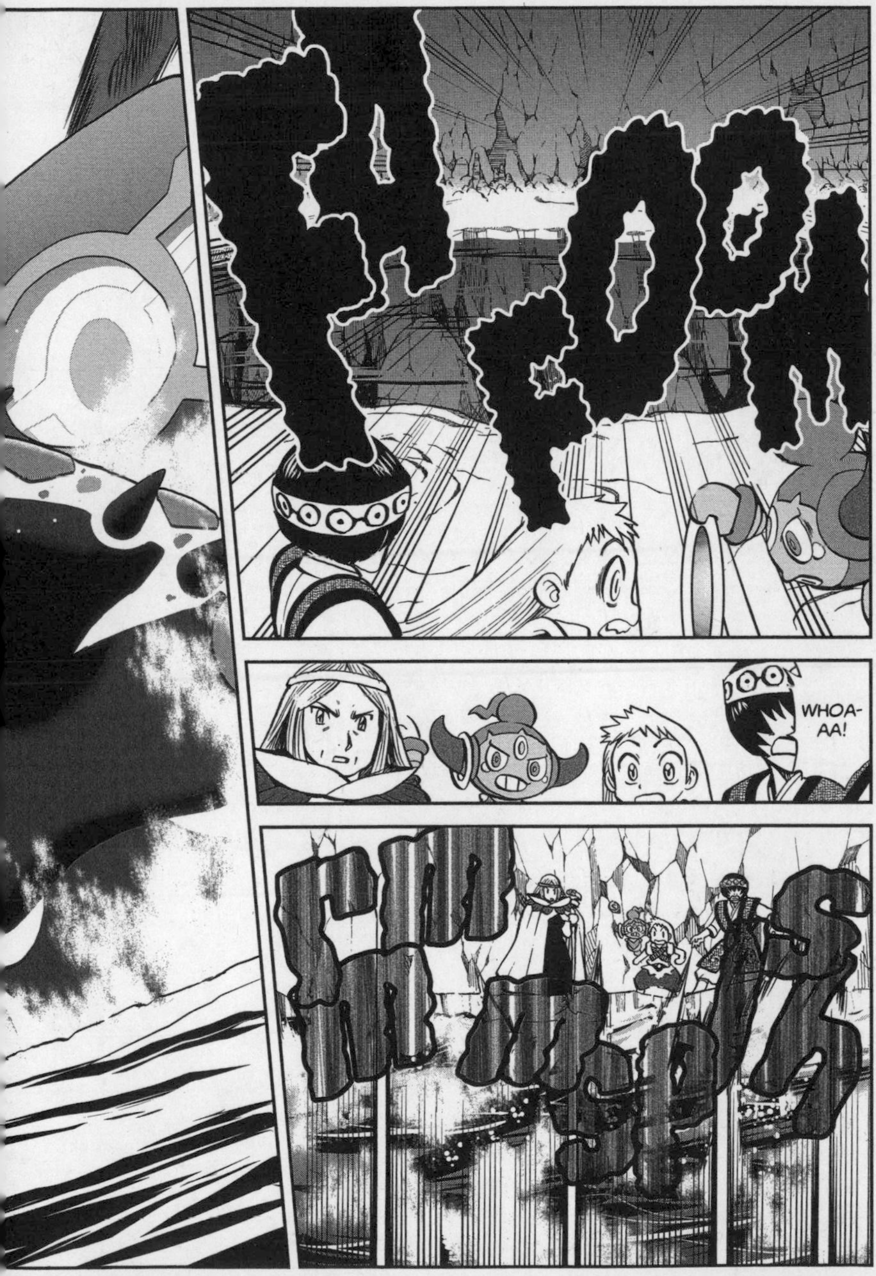
WHOA-AA!

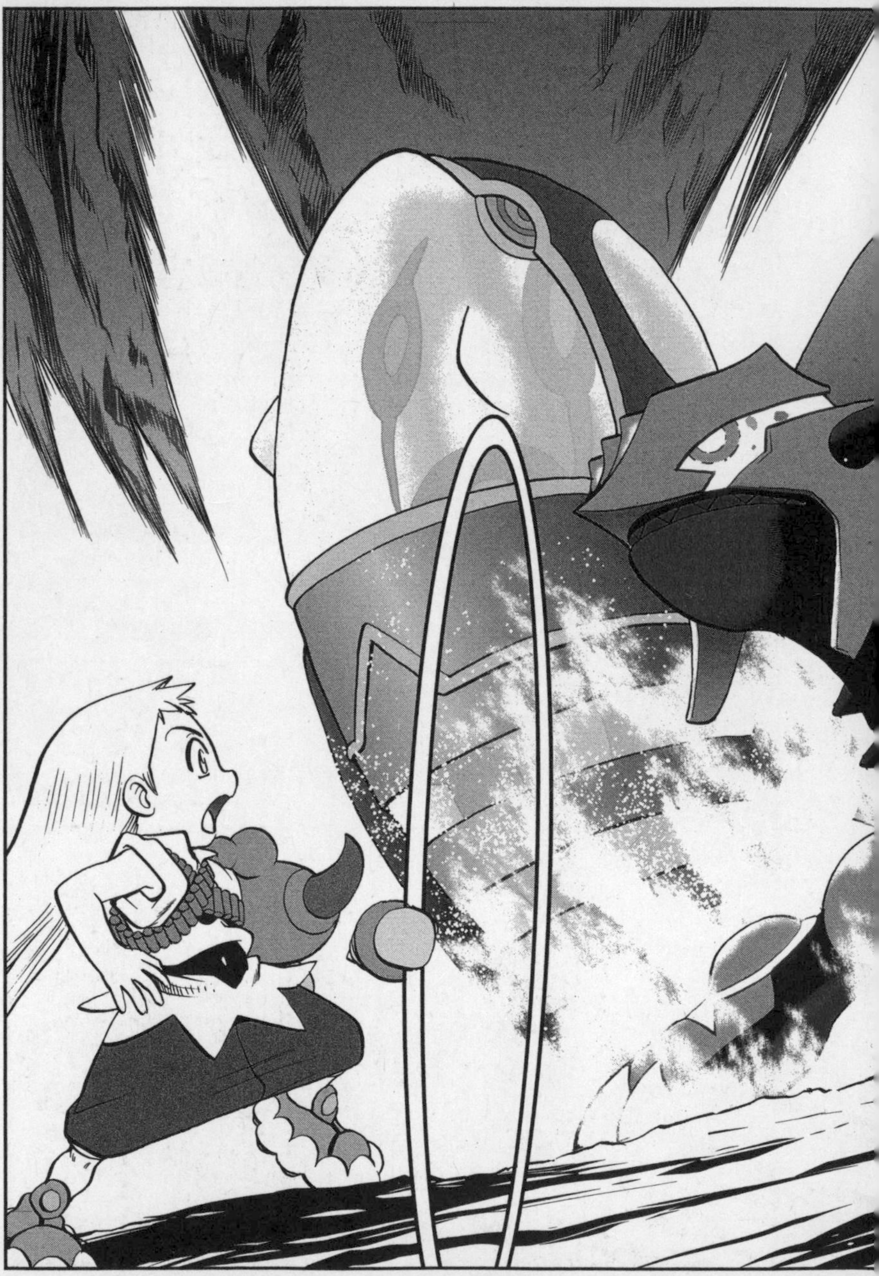

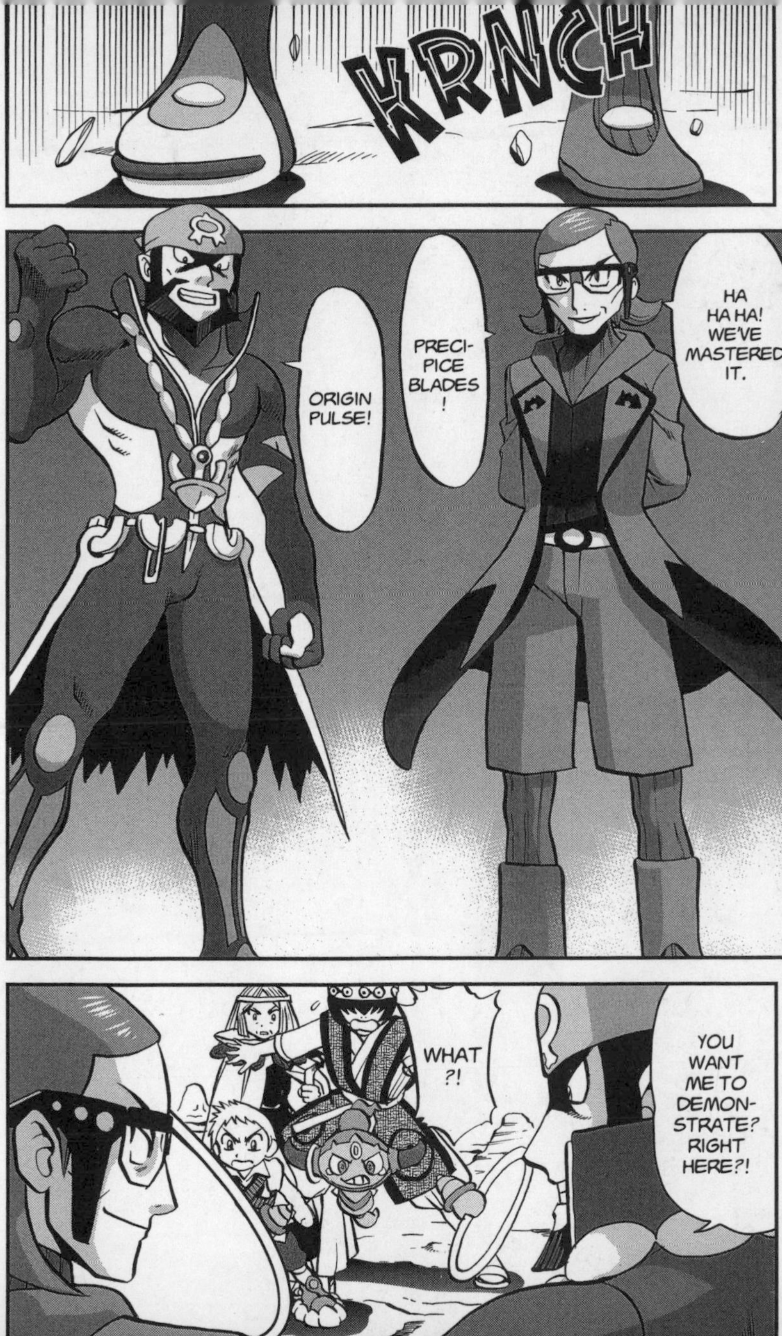
KRNCH
HA HA HA! WE'VE MASTERED IT.
PRECIPICE BLADES!
ORIGIN PULSE!
YOU WANT ME TO DEMONSTRATE? RIGHT HERE?!
WHAT?!

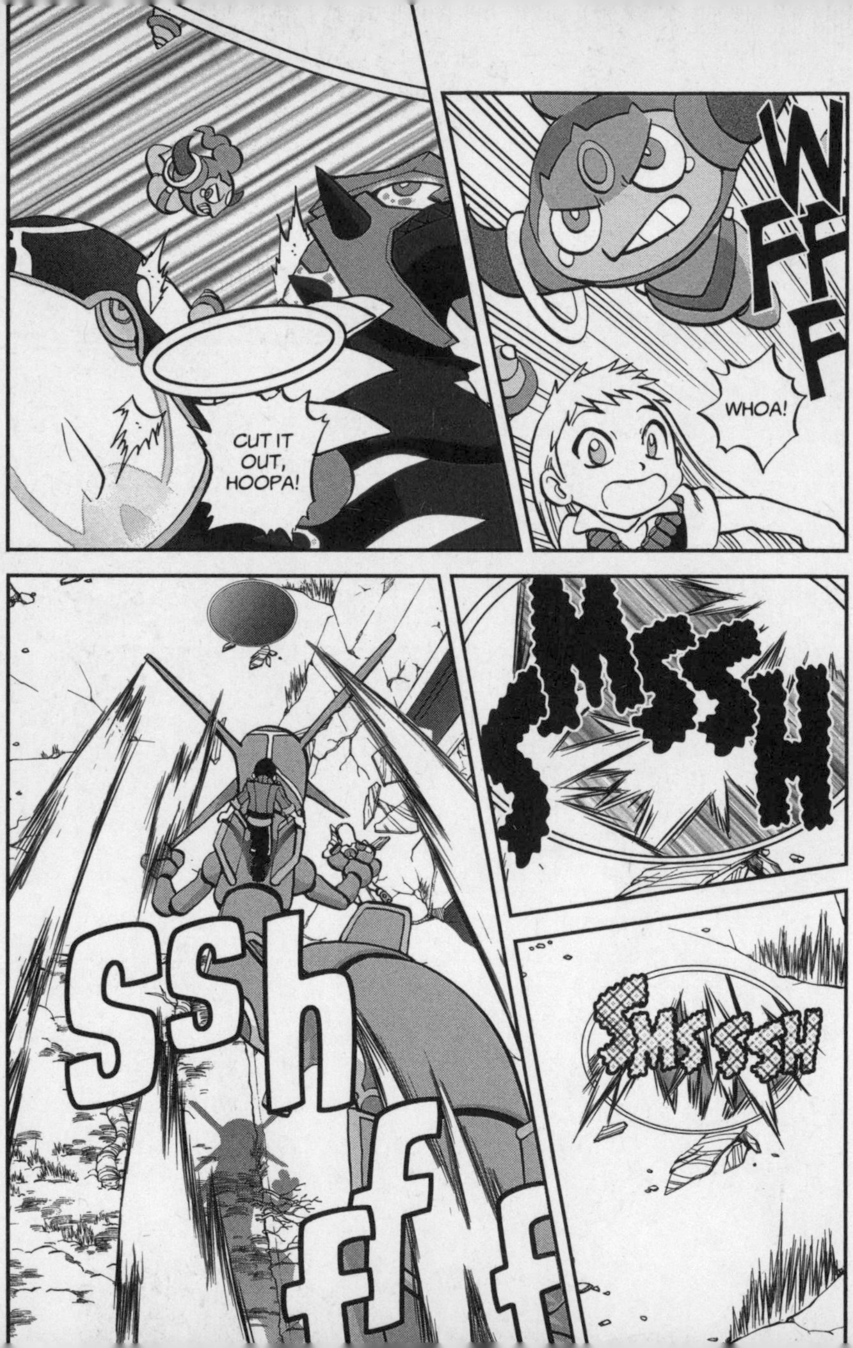
WFFF
WHOA!
CUT IT OUT, HOOPA!
SMSSH
SMSSSH
SSH
FFF

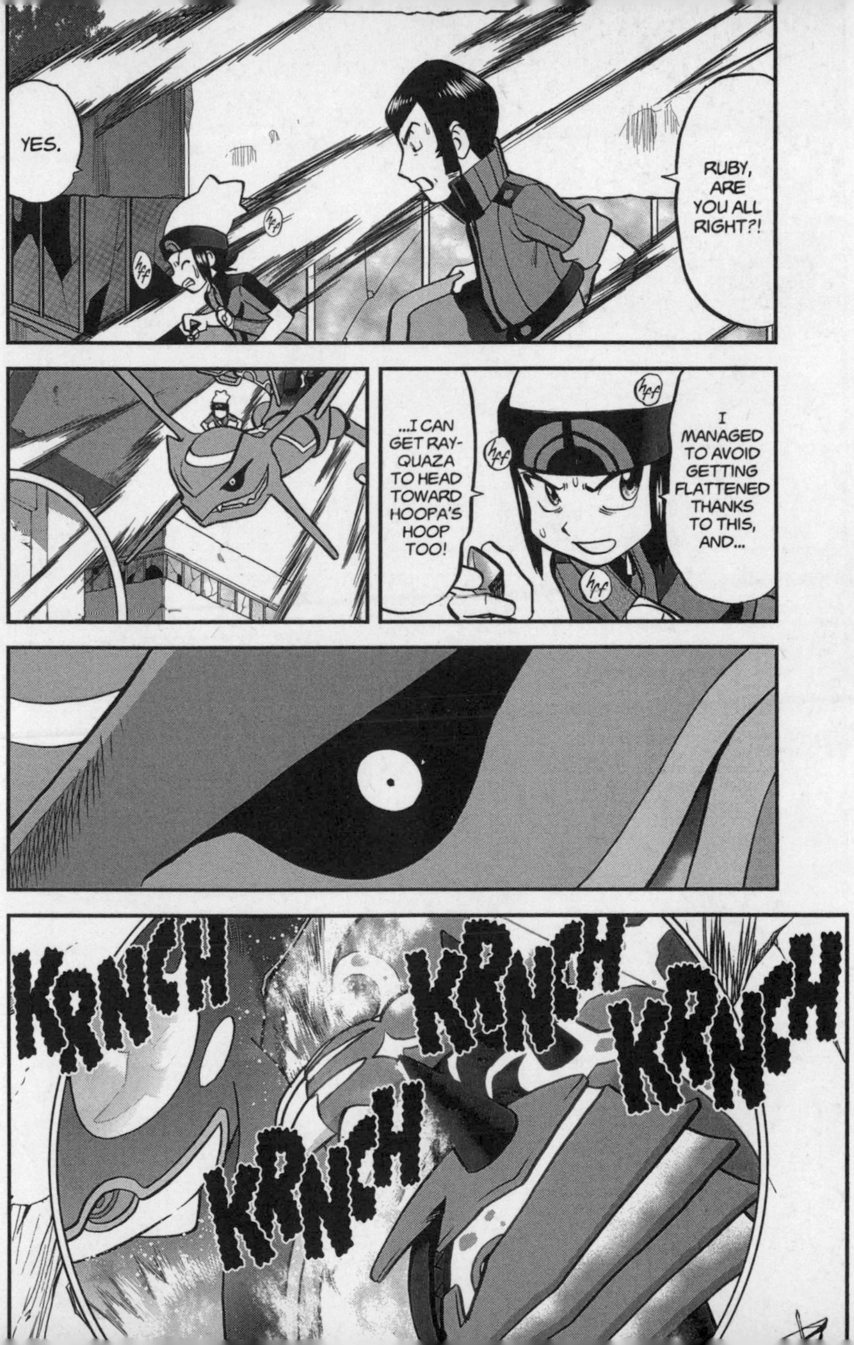
RUBY, ARE YOU ALL RIGHT?!
hff
hff
YES.
hff
I MANAGED TO AVOID GETTING FLATTENED THANKS TO THIS, AND...
hff
hff
...I CAN GET RAY-QUAZA TO HEAD TOWARD HOOPA'S HOOP TOO!
KRNCH
KRNCH
KRNCH
KRNCH

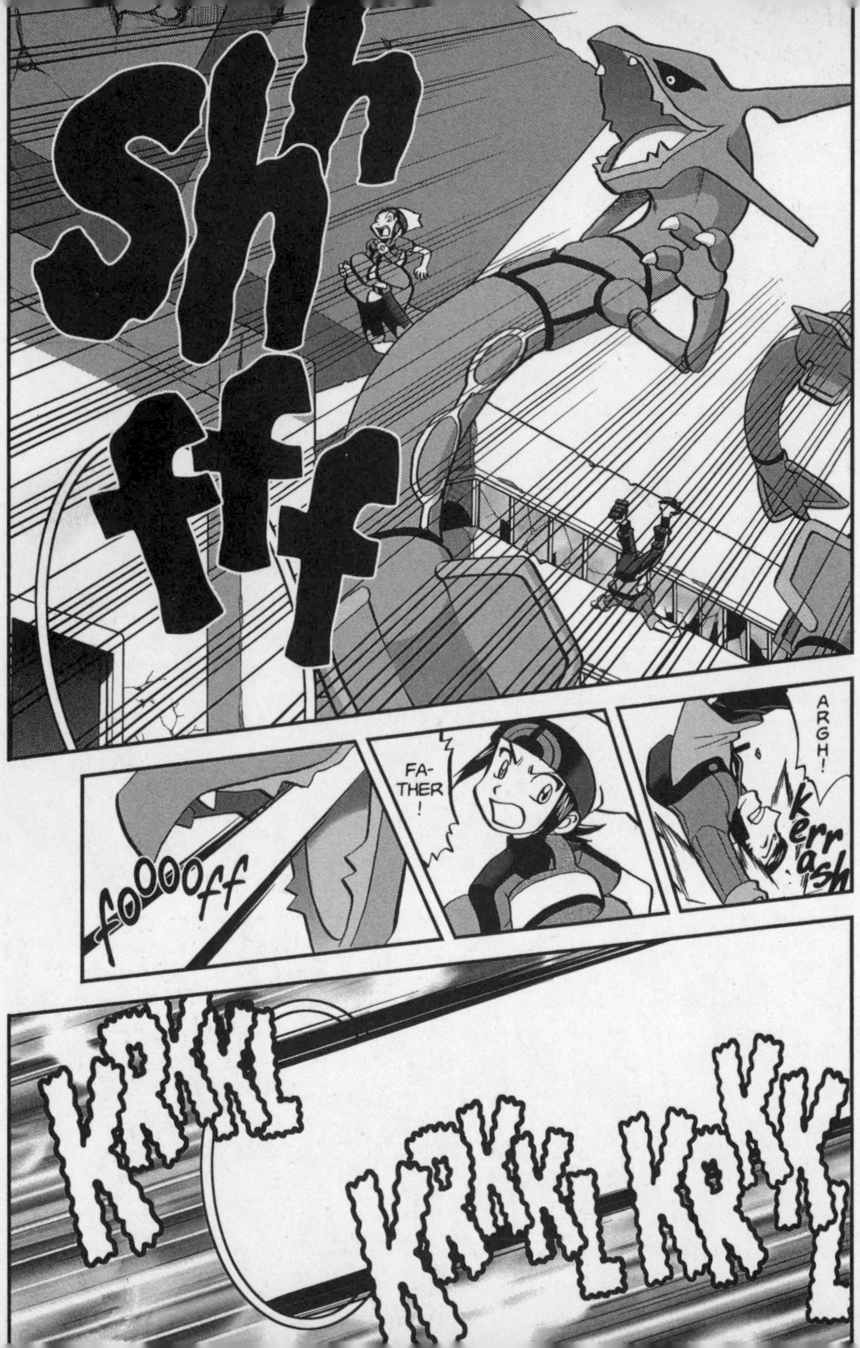
SHH
FFF
ARGH!
KERRASH
FA-THER!
FOOOOFF
KRKKL
KRKKL-KRKK

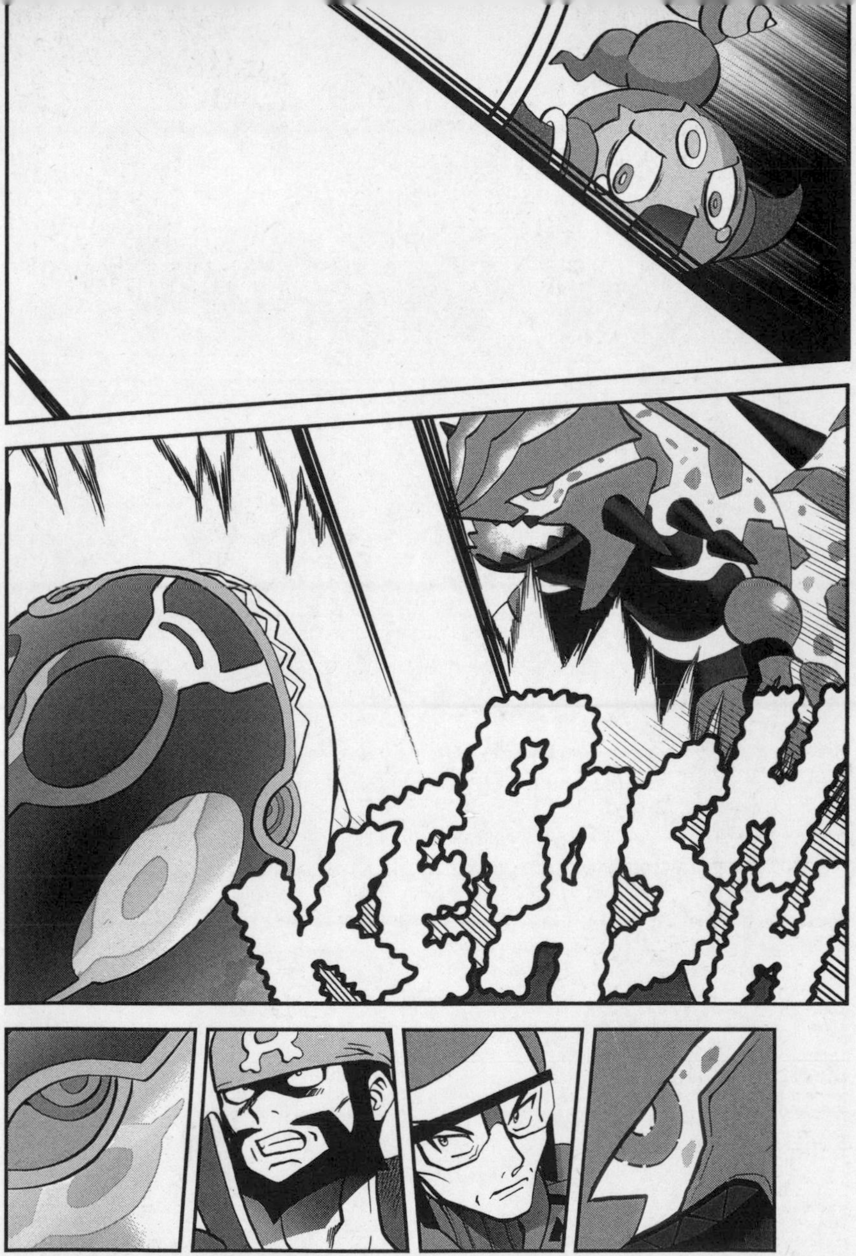
KRASH

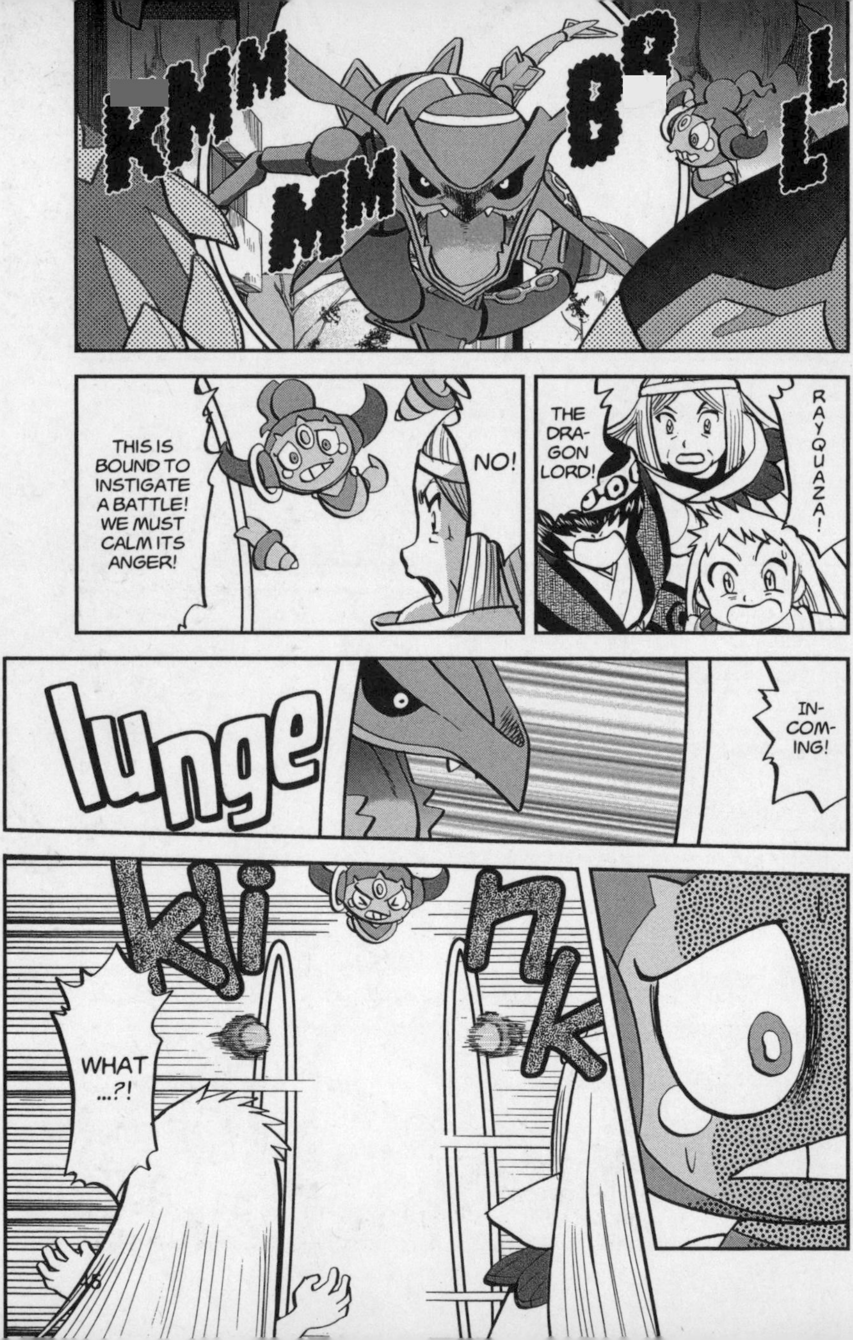
KMMMM
BRLL
RAYQUAZA!
THE DRAGON LORD!
NO!
THIS IS BOUND TO INSTIGATE A BATTLE! WE MUST CALM ITS ANGER!
INCOMING!
lunge
!
klink
WHAT ...?!

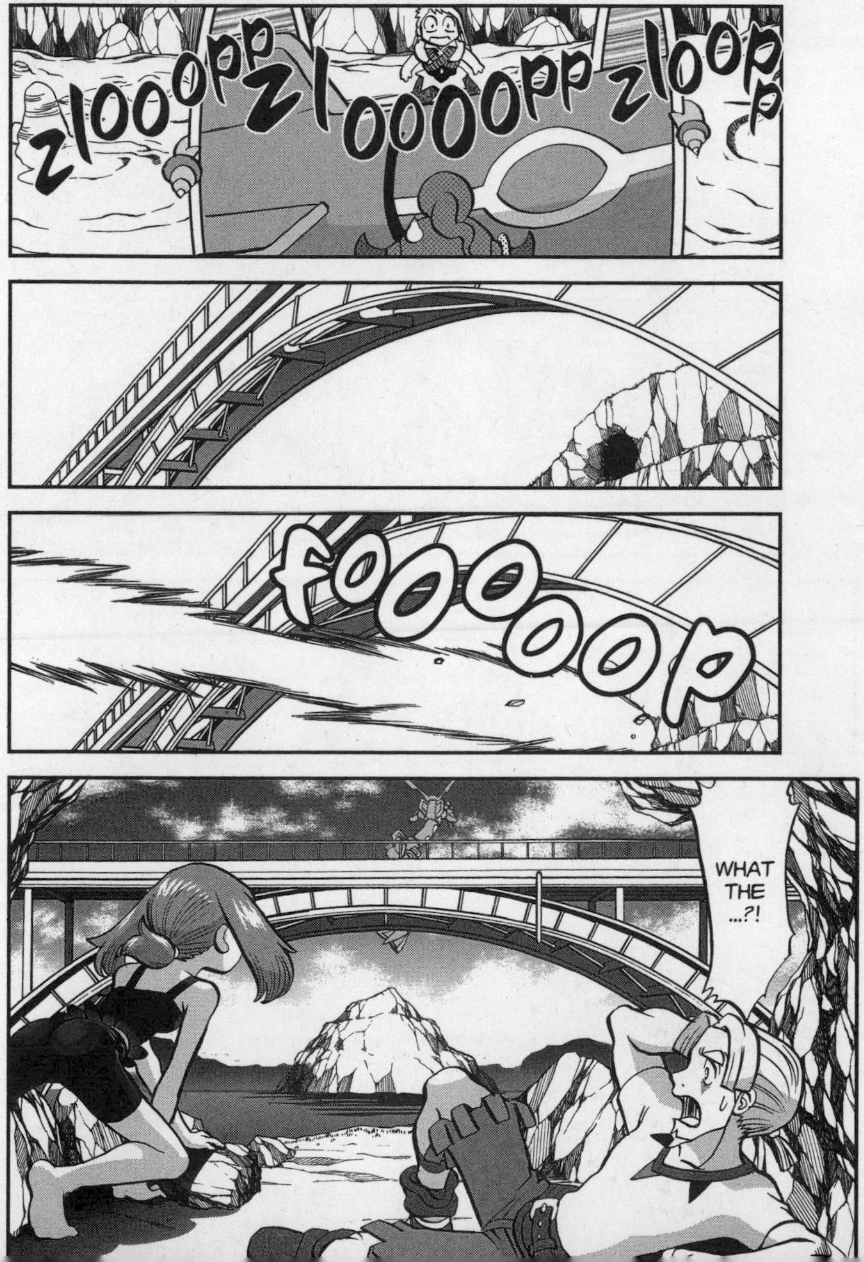
ZLOOOPP ZLOOOOOPP ZLOOPPP
FOOOOOP
WHAT THE ...?!

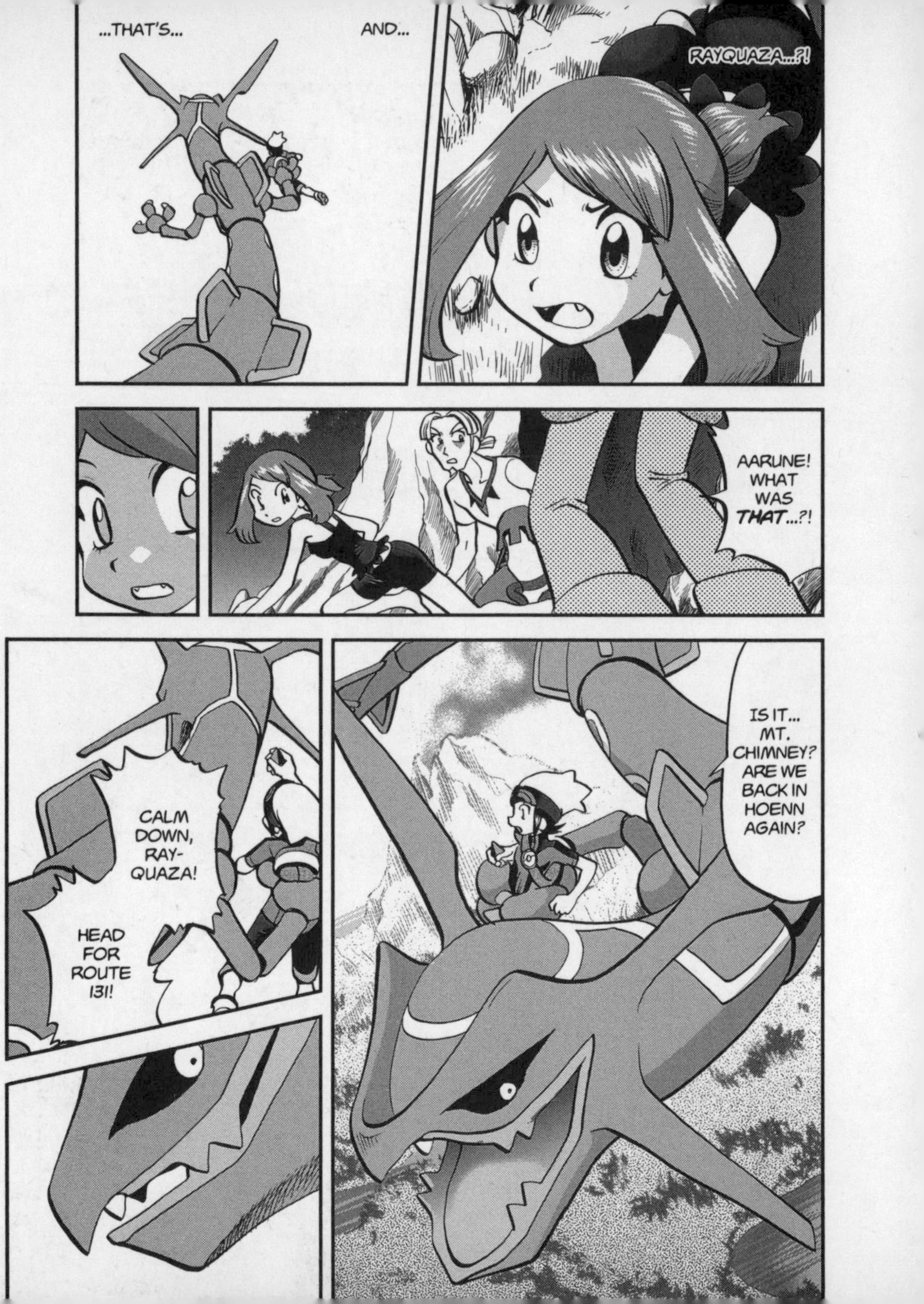
RAYQUAZA...?!
AND...
...THAT'S...
AARUNE! WHAT WAS *THAT*...?!
IS IT... MT. CHIMNEY? ARE WE BACK IN HOENN AGAIN?
CALM DOWN, RAY-QUAZA!
HEAD FOR ROUTE 131!

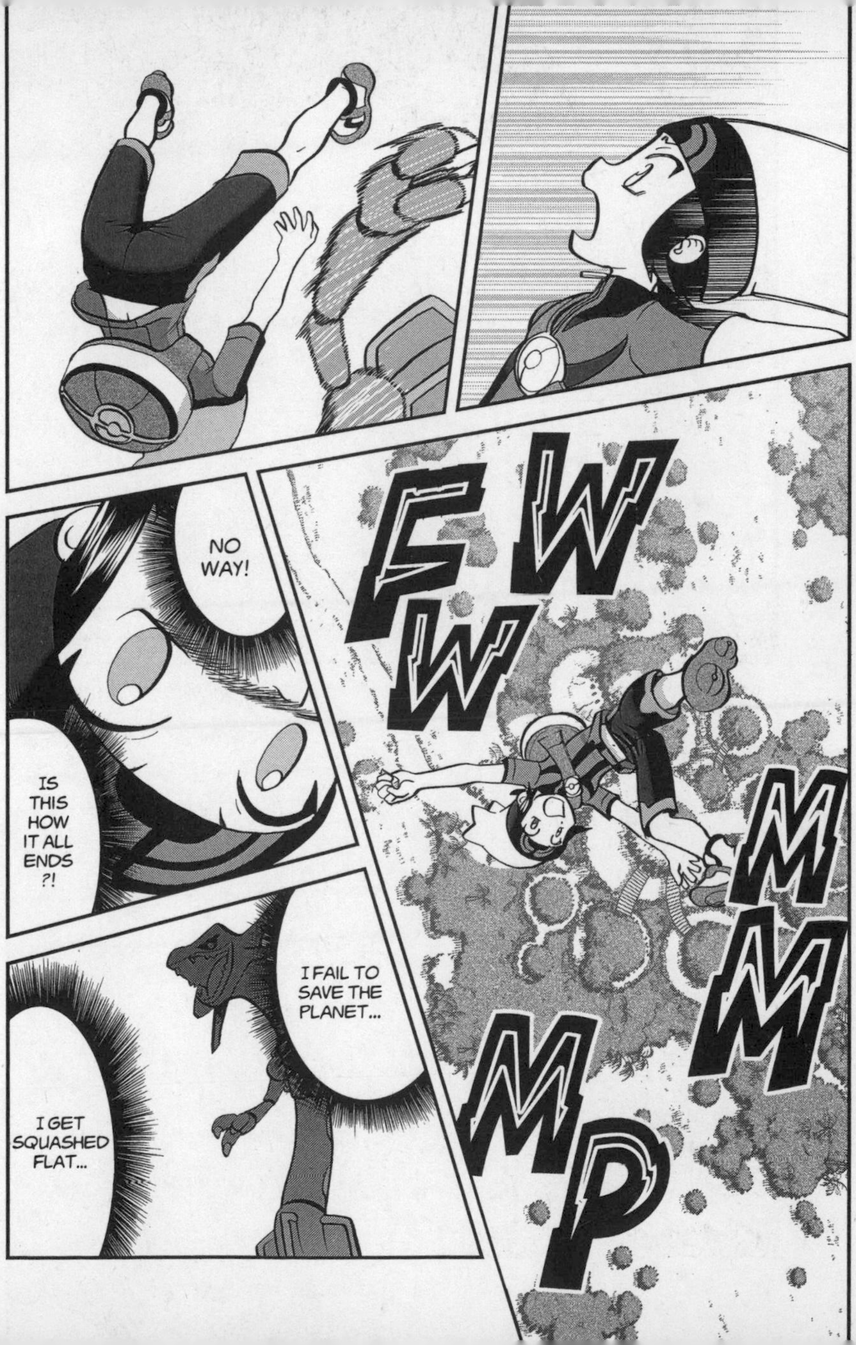
FWW
MMMMP
NO WAY!
IS THIS HOW IT ALL ENDS?!
I FAIL TO SAVE THE PLANET...
I GET SQUASHED FLAT...

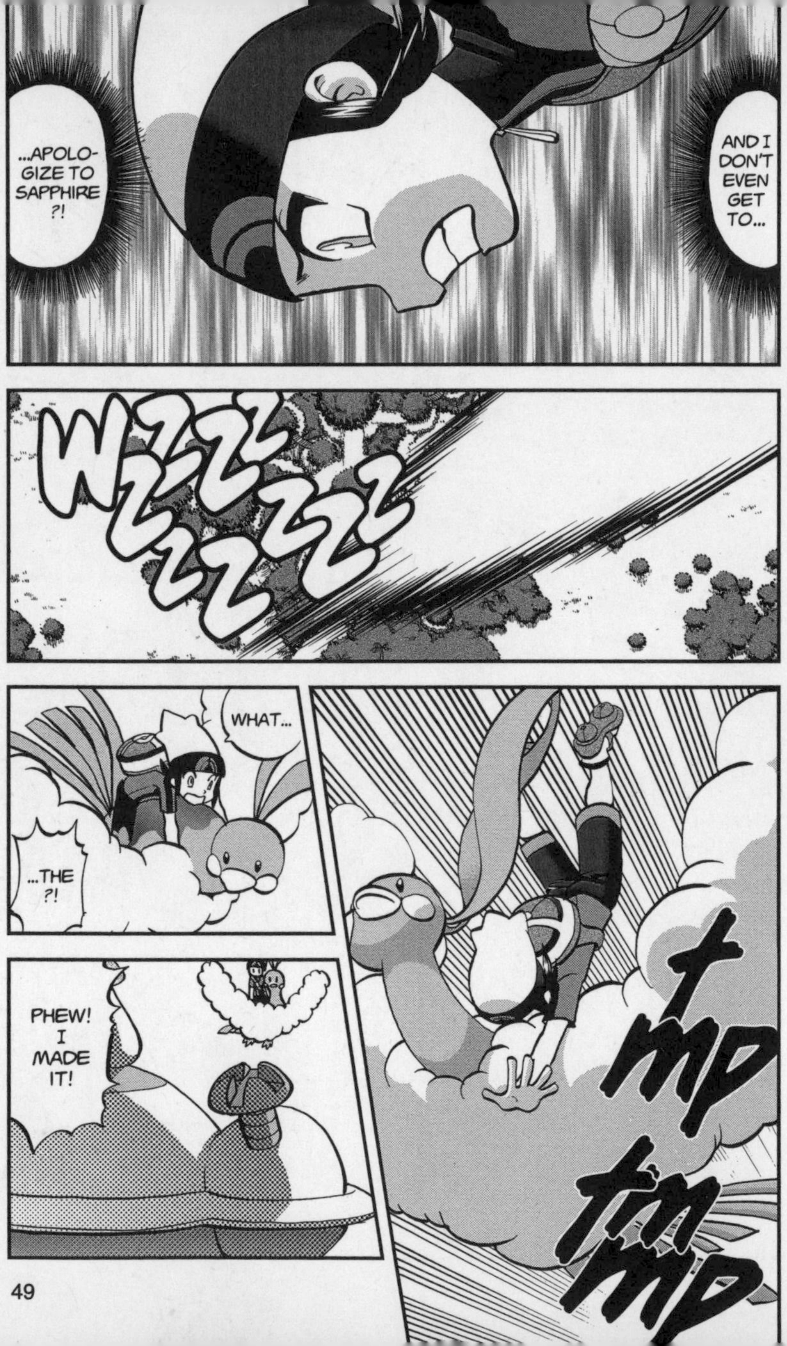
AND I DON'T EVEN GET TO...
...APOLOGIZE TO SAPPHIRE ?!
WZZZZZZZZZ
TMP TMP TMP
WHAT...
...THE ?!
PHEW! I MADE IT!

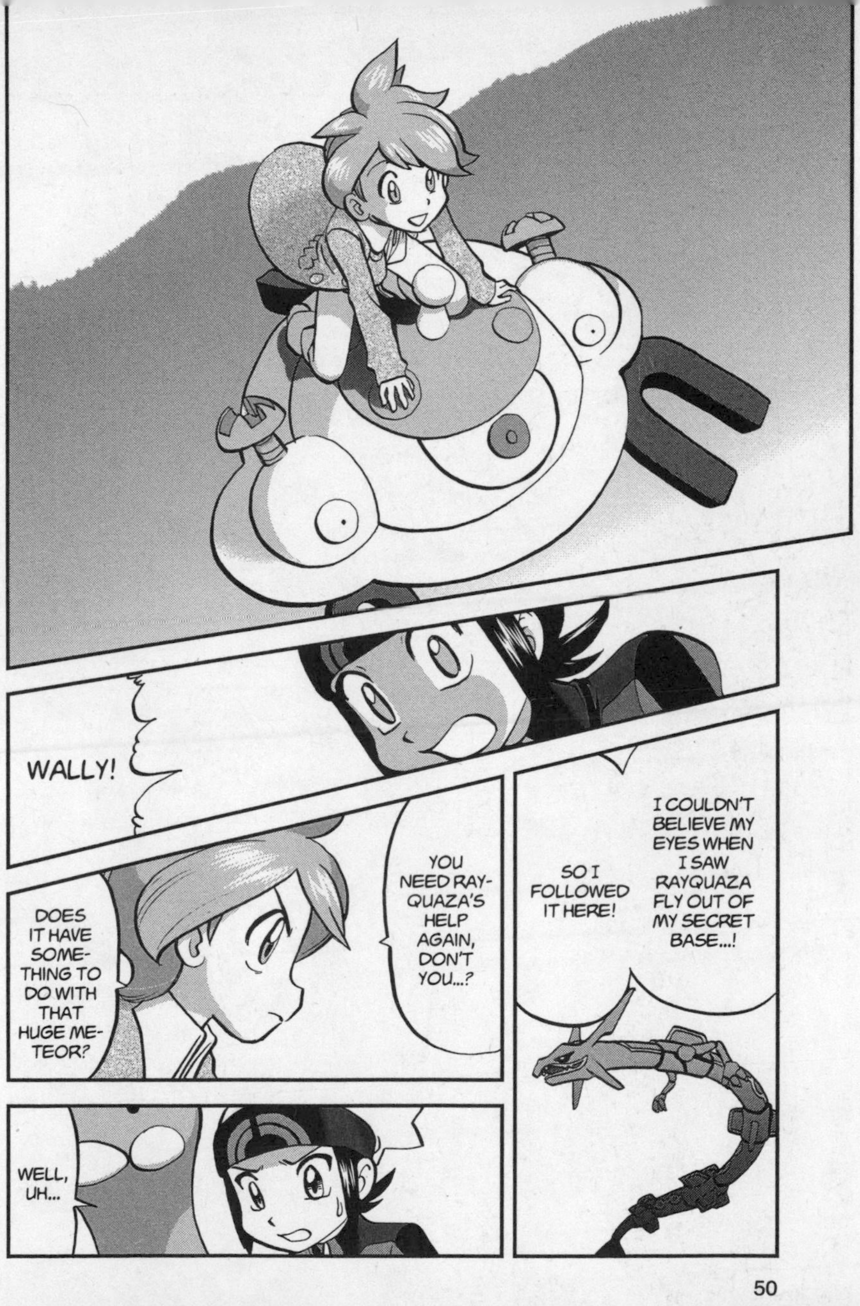

WALLY!
I COULDN'T BELIEVE MY EYES WHEN I SAW RAYQUAZA FLY OUT OF MY SECRET BASE...!
SO I FOLLOWED IT HERE!
YOU NEED RAYQUAZA'S HELP AGAIN, DON'T YOU...?
DOES IT HAVE SOMETHING TO DO WITH THAT HUGE METEOR?
WELL, UH...

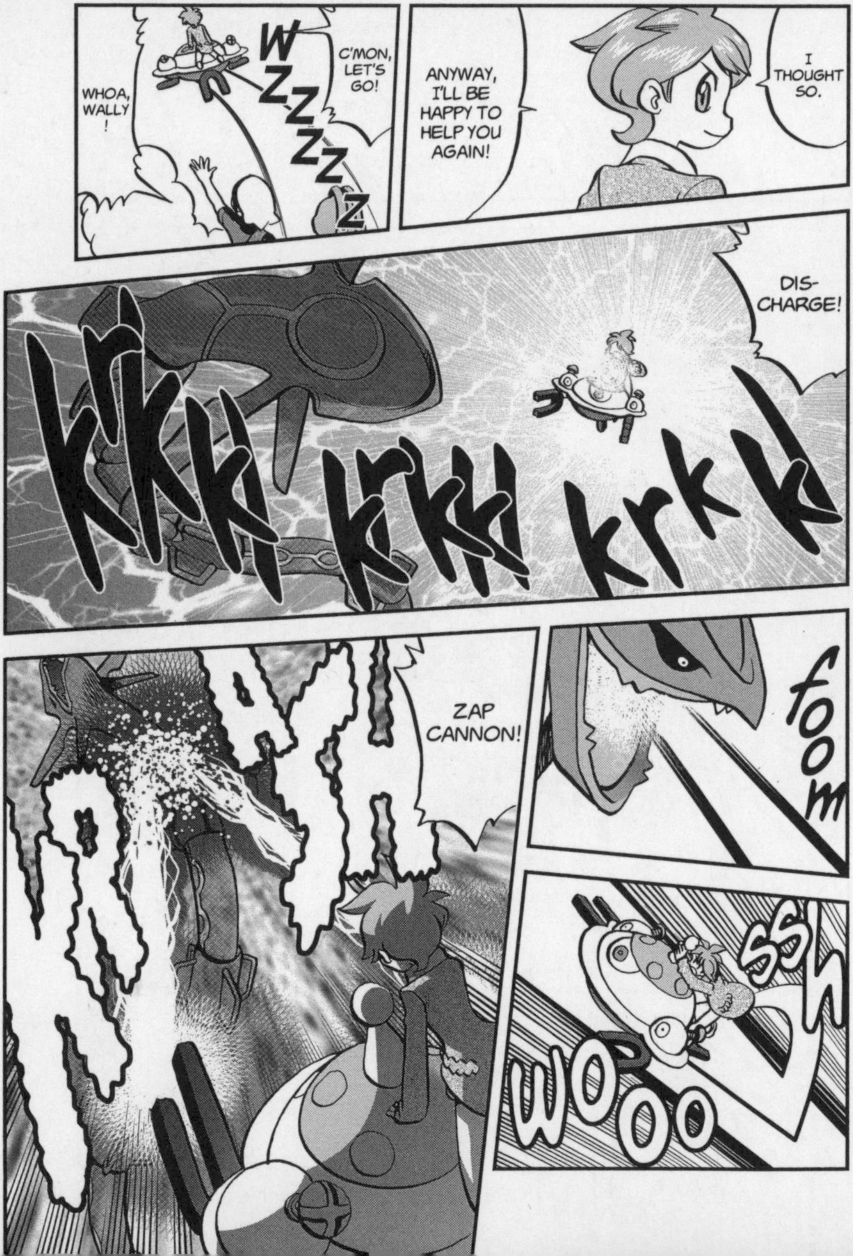
I THOUGHT SO.
ANYWAY, I'LL BE HAPPY TO HELP YOU AGAIN!
C'MON, LET'S GO!
WZZZZZZ
WHOA, WALLY!
DIS-CHARGE!
foom
WOOO SSH
ZAP CANNON!

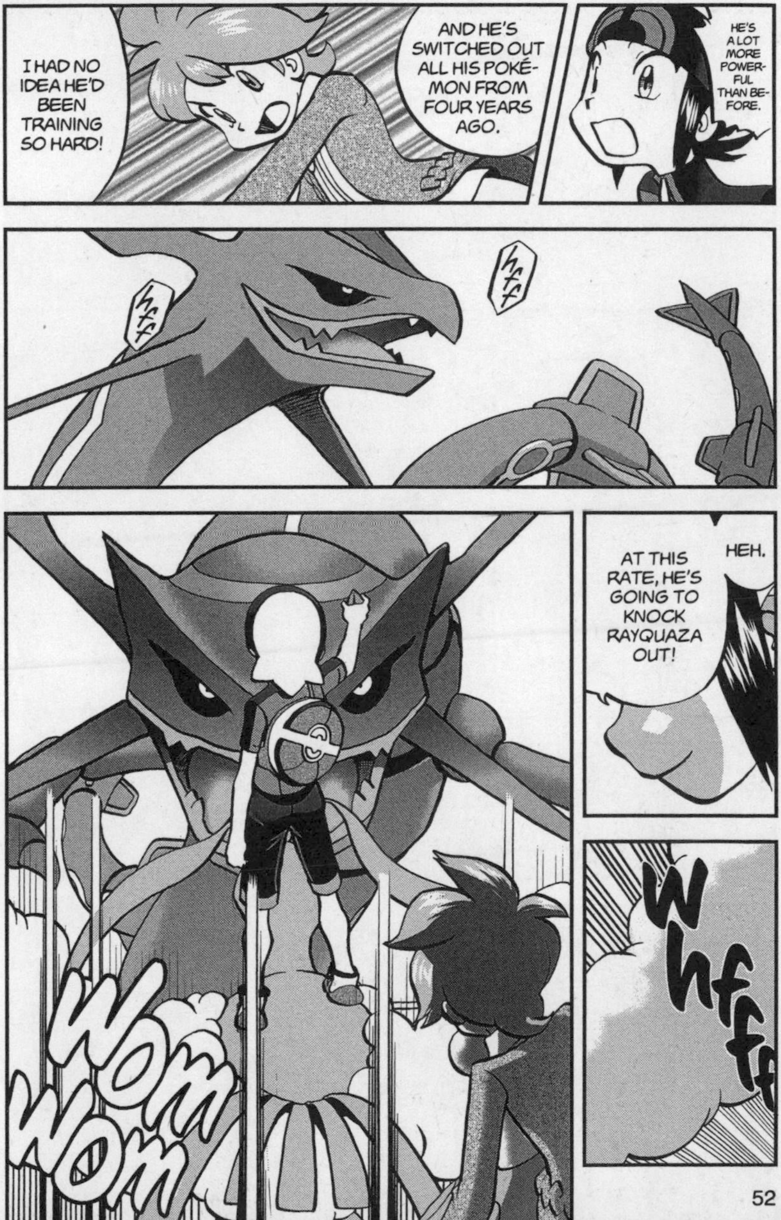
HE'S A LOT MORE POWER-FUL THAN BE-FORE.
AND HE'S SWITCHED OUT ALL HIS POKÉ-MON FROM FOUR YEARS AGO.
I HAD NO IDEA HE'D BEEN TRAINING SO HARD!
hff
hff
HEH.
AT THIS RATE, HE'S GOING TO KNOCK RAYQUAZA OUT!
Whfff
WOM WOM

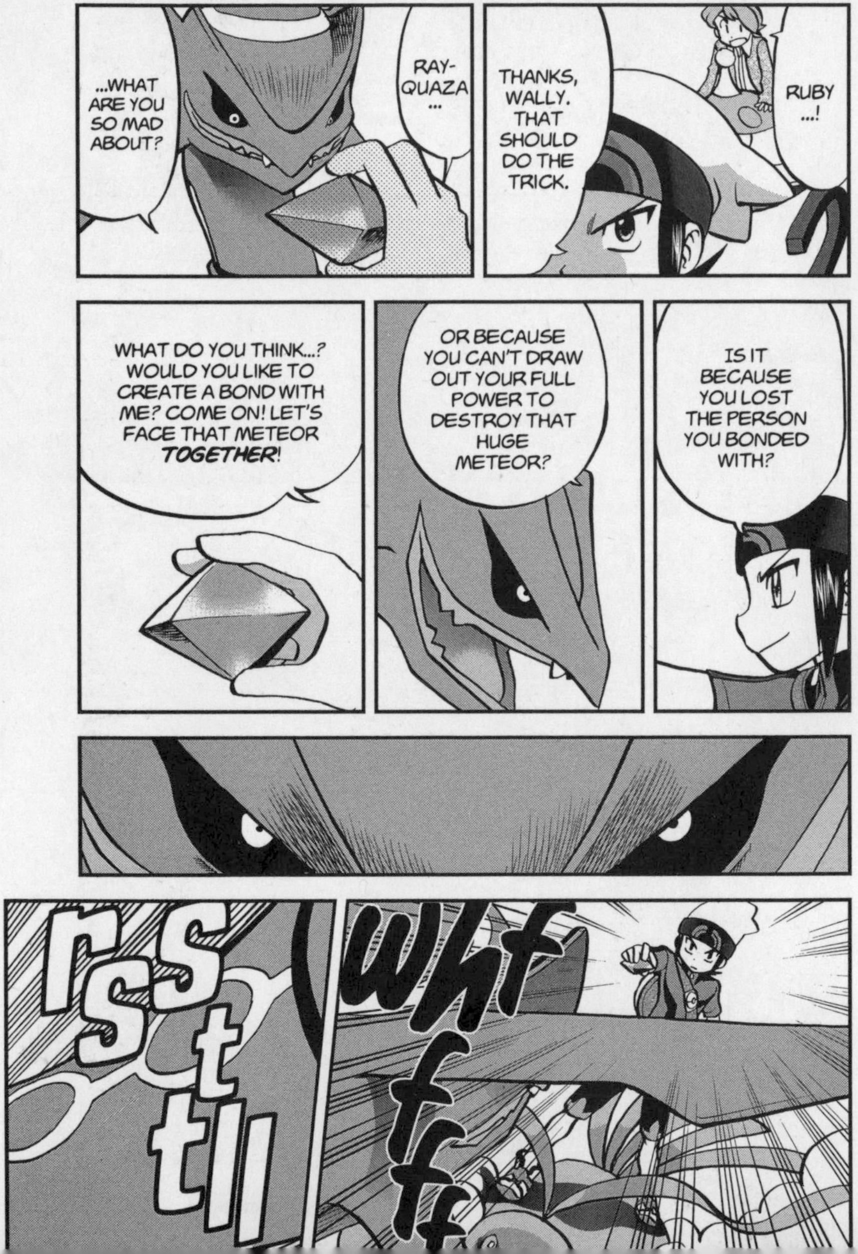
RUBY ...!
THANKS, WALLY. THAT SHOULD DO THE TRICK.
RAY-QUAZA ...
...WHAT ARE YOU SO MAD ABOUT?
IS IT BECAUSE YOU LOST THE PERSON YOU BONDED WITH?
OR BECAUSE YOU CAN'T DRAW OUT YOUR FULL POWER TO DESTROY THAT HUGE METEOR?
WHAT DO YOU THINK...? WOULD YOU LIKE TO CREATE A BOND WITH ME? COME ON! LET'S FACE THAT METEOR *TOGETHER*!
whf
ffff
rsS
S
t
tll

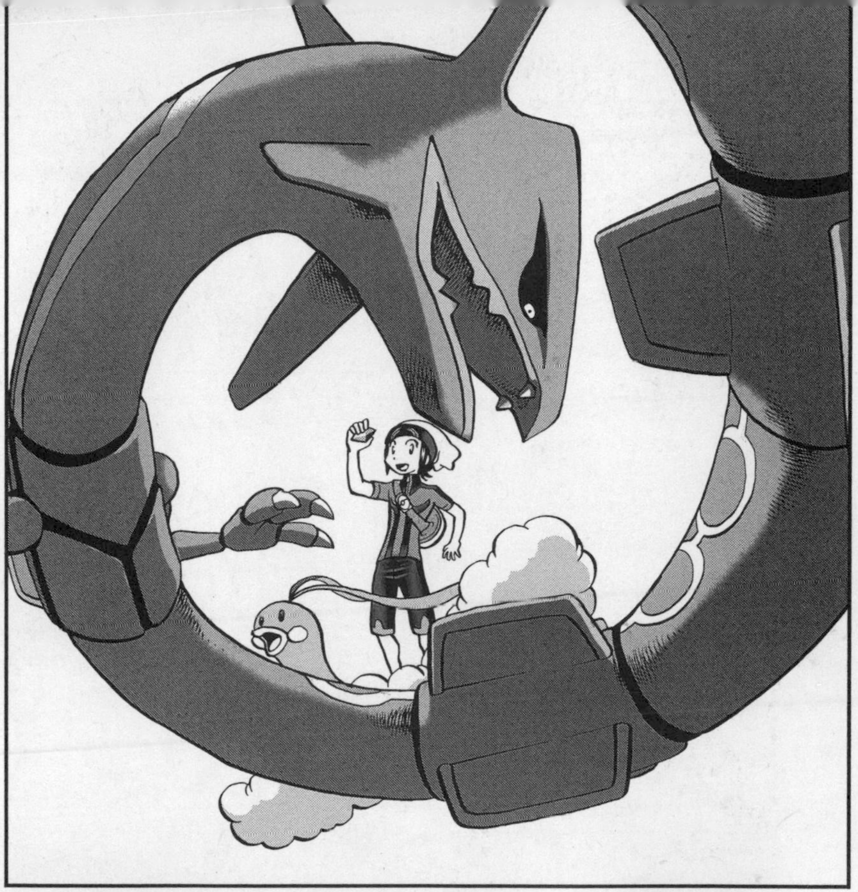

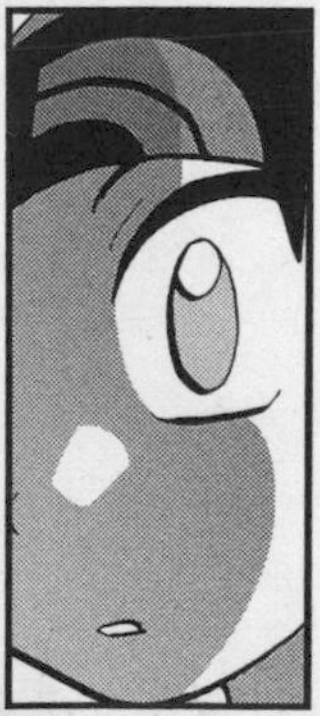

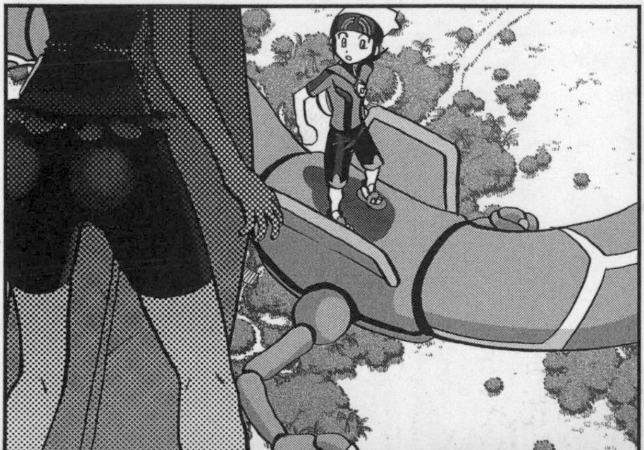

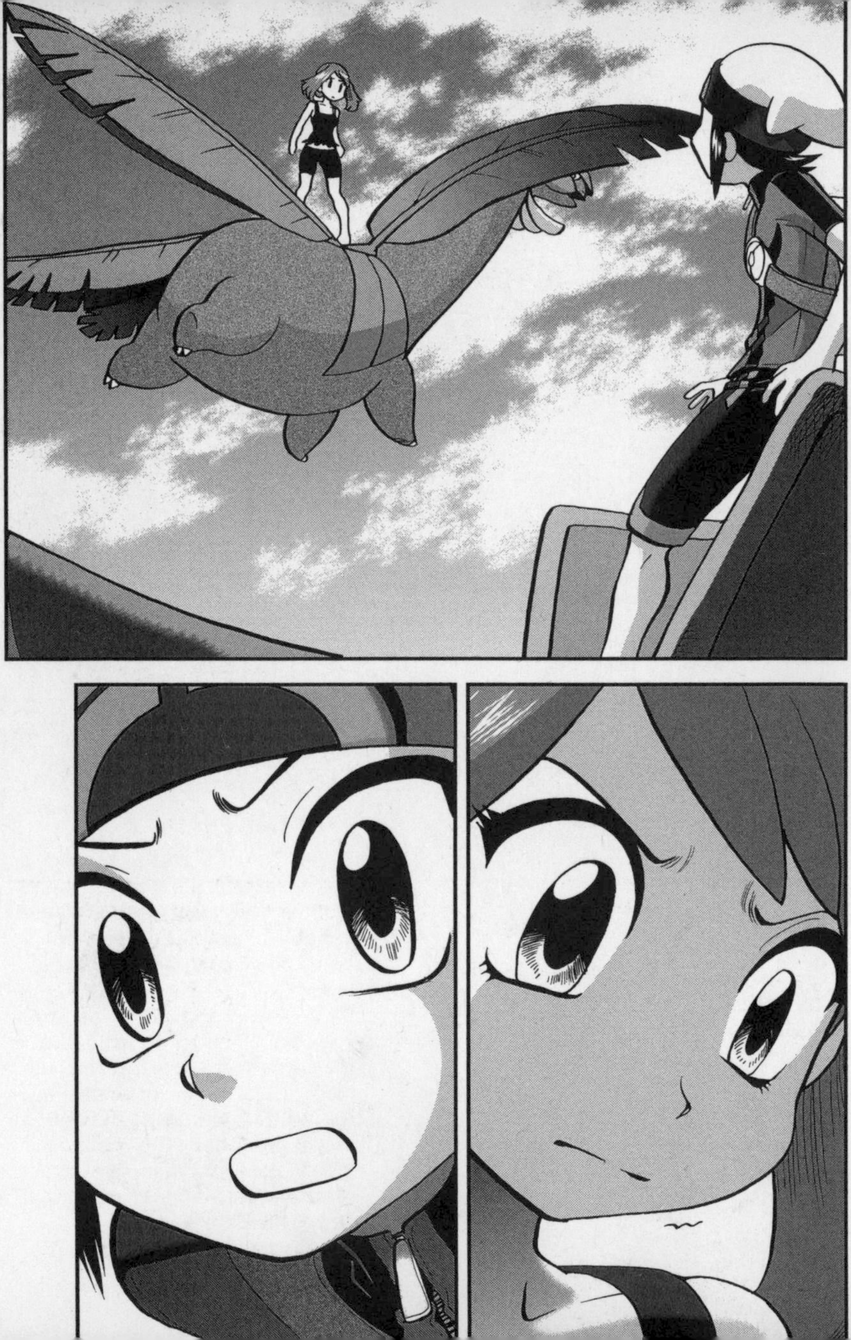

FRONTIER BRAIN

Skilled Trainers who protect each of the battle facilities at the Battle Frontier. The Hoenn Battle Frontier has seven facilities called the Battle Tower, Battle Dome, Battle Pyramid, Battle Pike, Battle Arena, Battle Palace and Battle Factory. The seven Frontier Brains will face the challenger at each of those facilities. Each facility has a unique rule and it is extremely difficult to defeat them, but if the challenger manages to beat them, they are rewarded with a Frontier Symbol. The Battle Frontier exists in other regions as well.

Omega Alpha Adventure 17

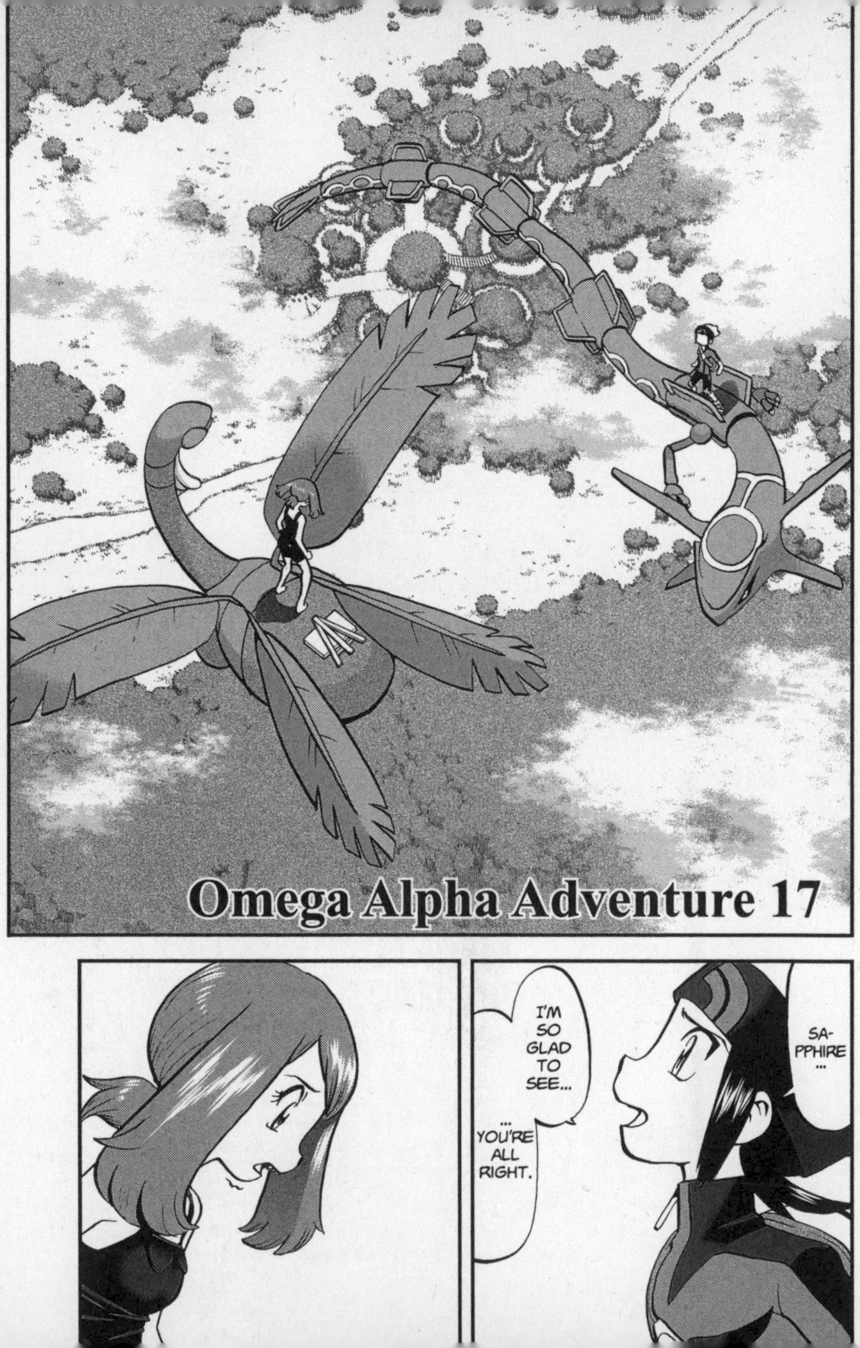
SA-
PPHIRE
...
I'M SO GLAD TO SEE...
... YOU'RE ALL RIGHT.

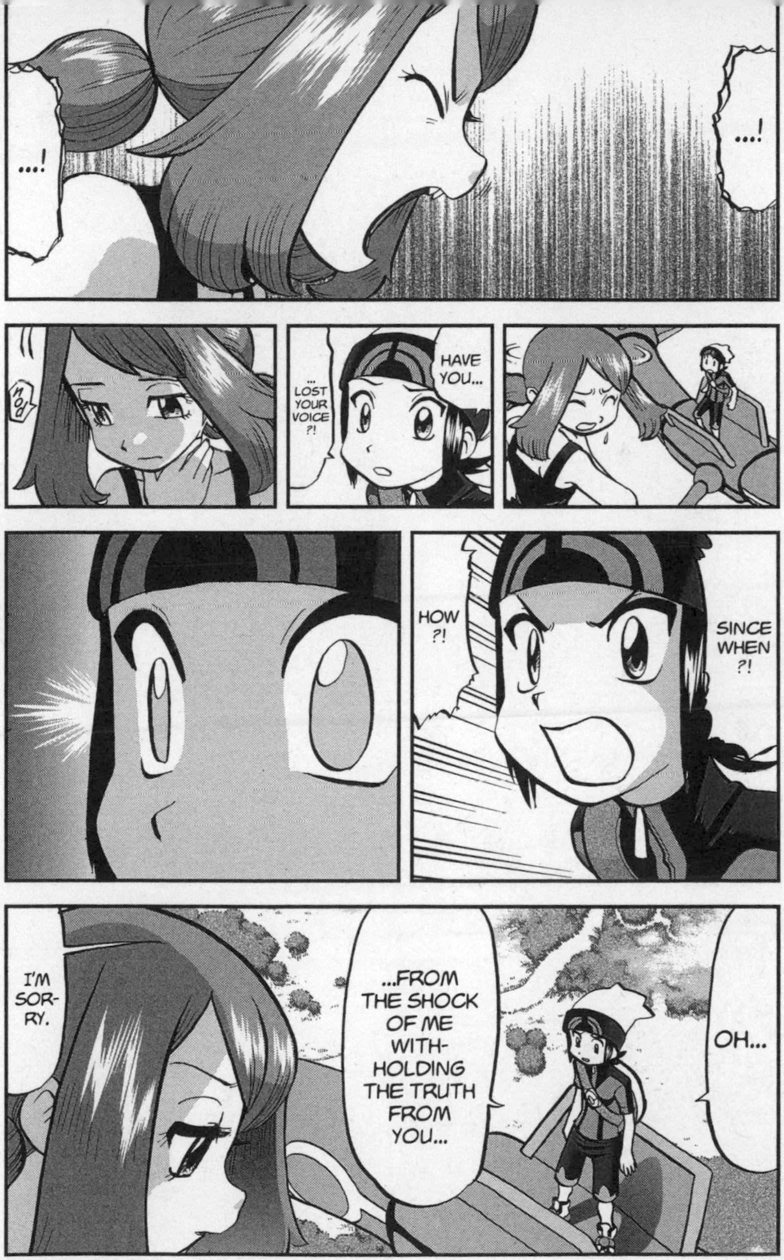
...!
...!
HAVE YOU...
...LOST YOUR VOICE ?!
nod
SINCE WHEN ?!
HOW ?!
OH...
...FROM THE SHOCK OF ME WITH-HOLDING THE TRUTH FROM YOU...
I'M SOR-RY.

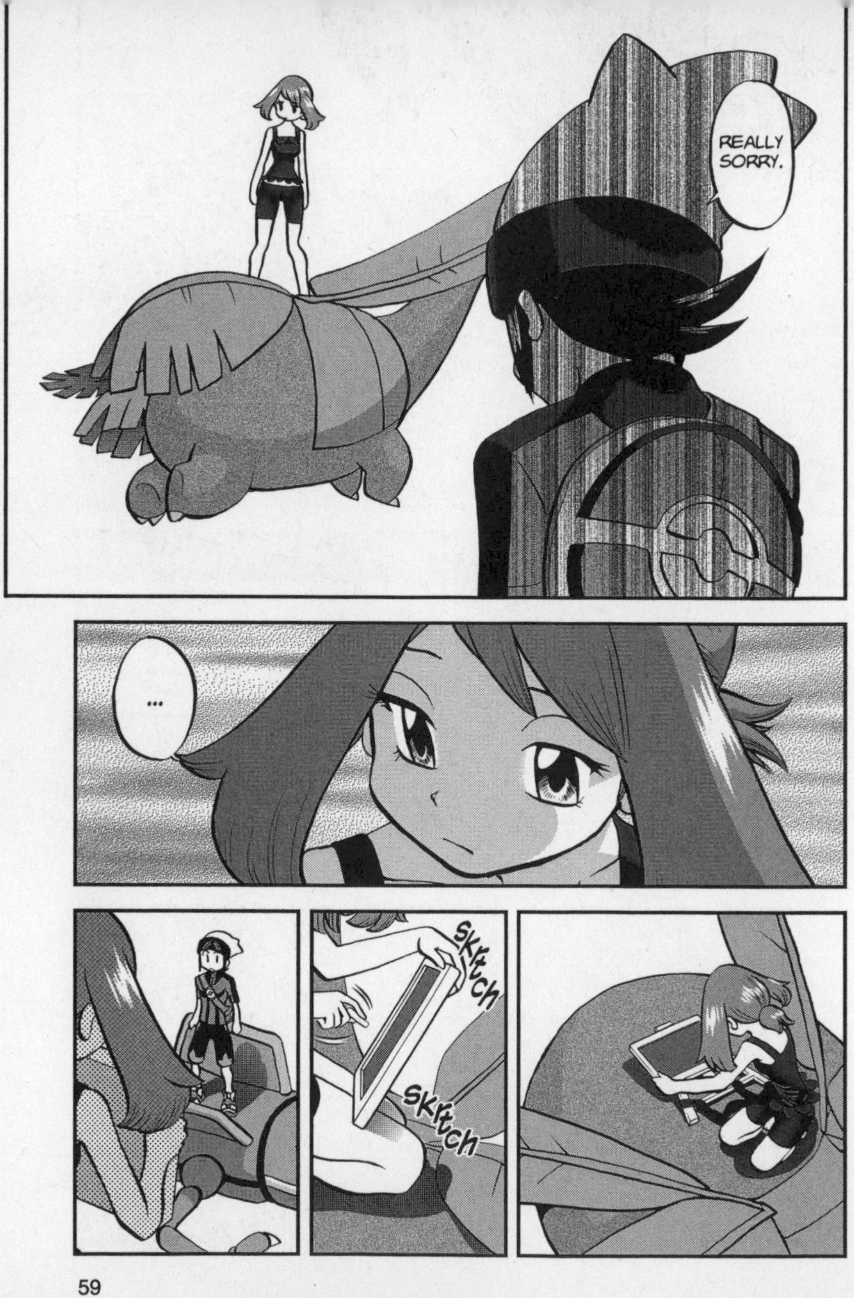
REALLY SORRY.
...
SKRTCH
SKRTCH

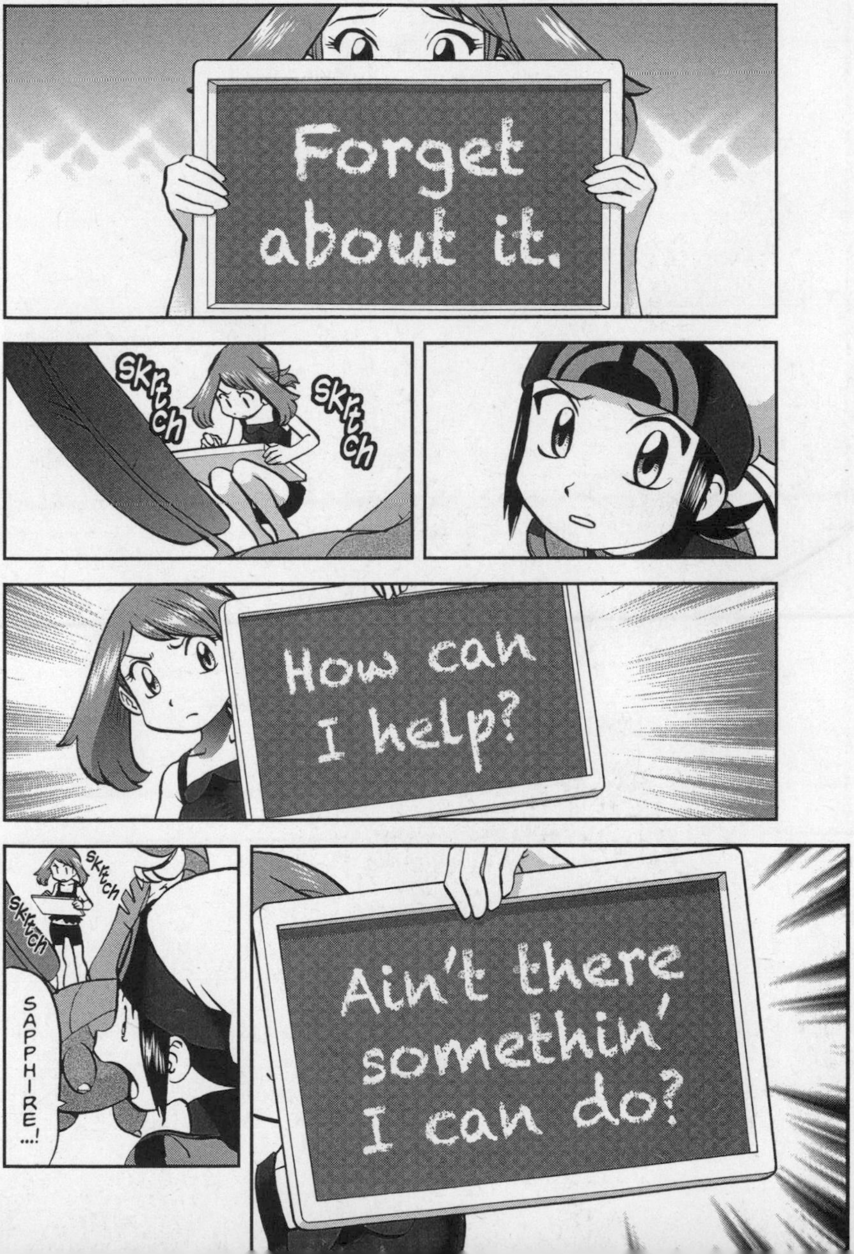
Forget about it.
SKRTCH
SKRTCH
How can I help?
Ain't there somethin' I can do?
SKRTCH
SKRTCH
SAPPHIRE...!

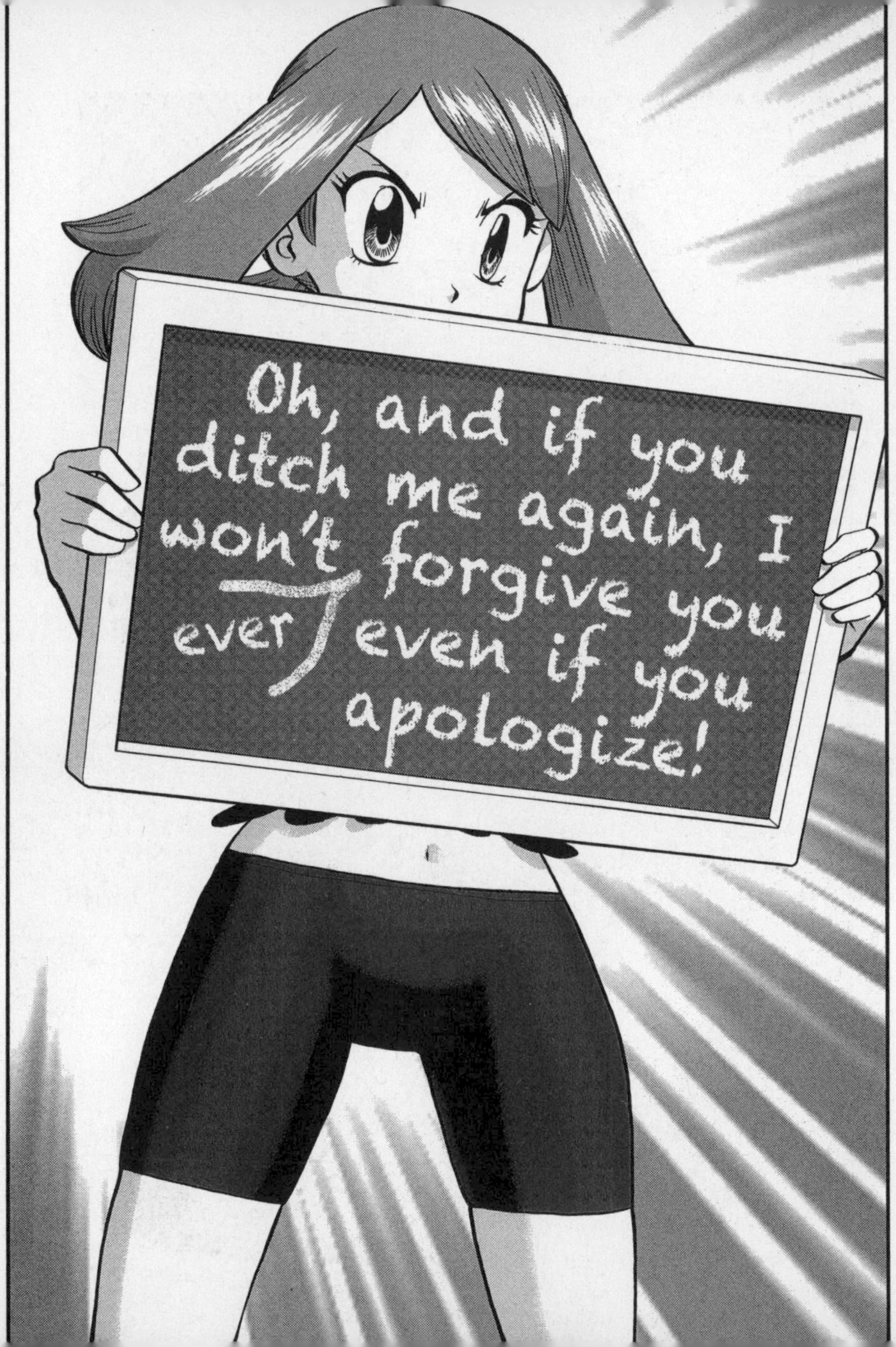
Oh, and if you ditch me again, I won't forgive you ever even if you apologize!

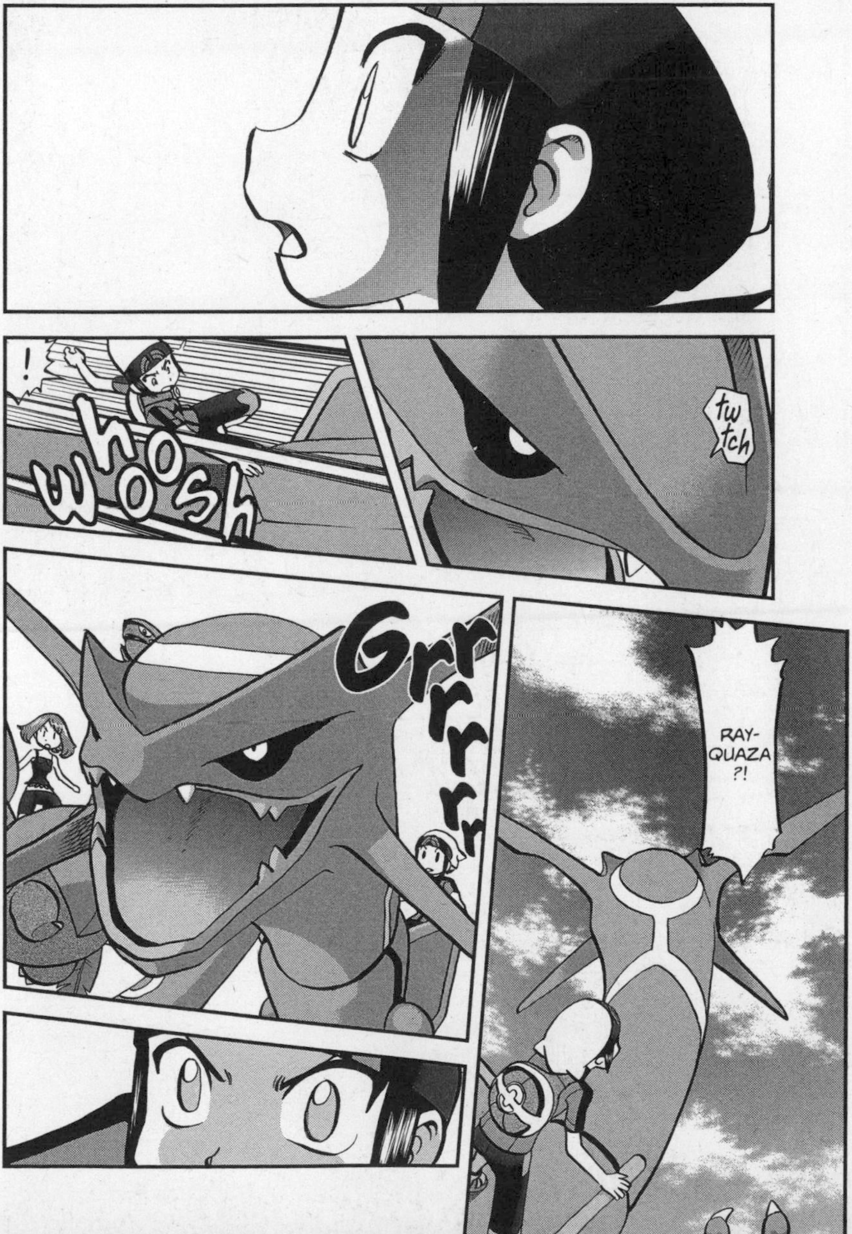
tw tch
!
whoosh
RAY-QUAZA?!
Grrrrrr

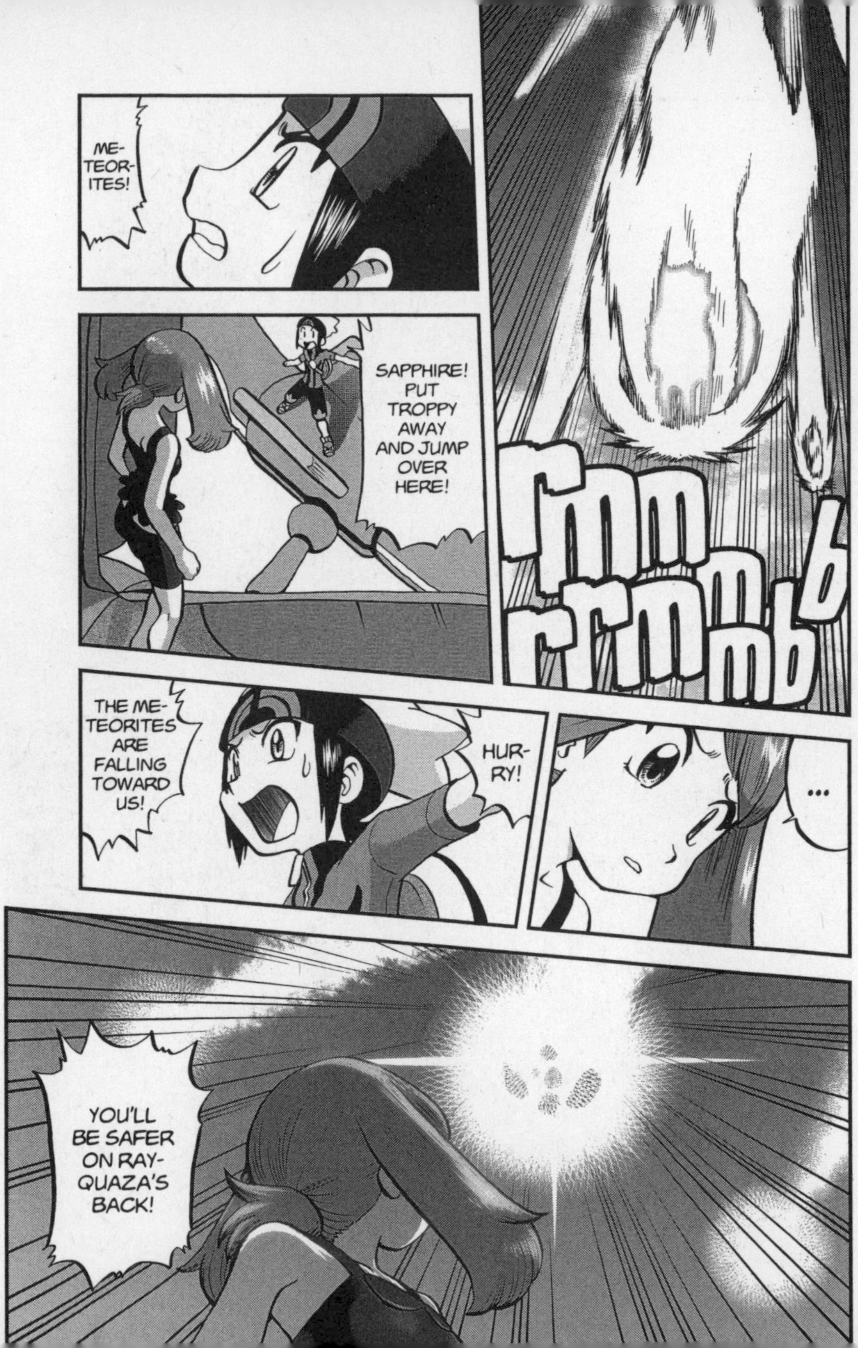
ME-TEORITES!
SAPPHIRE! PUT TROPPY AWAY AND JUMP OVER HERE!
...
THE ME-TEORITES ARE FALLING TOWARD US!
HUR-RY!
YOU'LL BE SAFER ON RAY-QUAZA'S BACK!

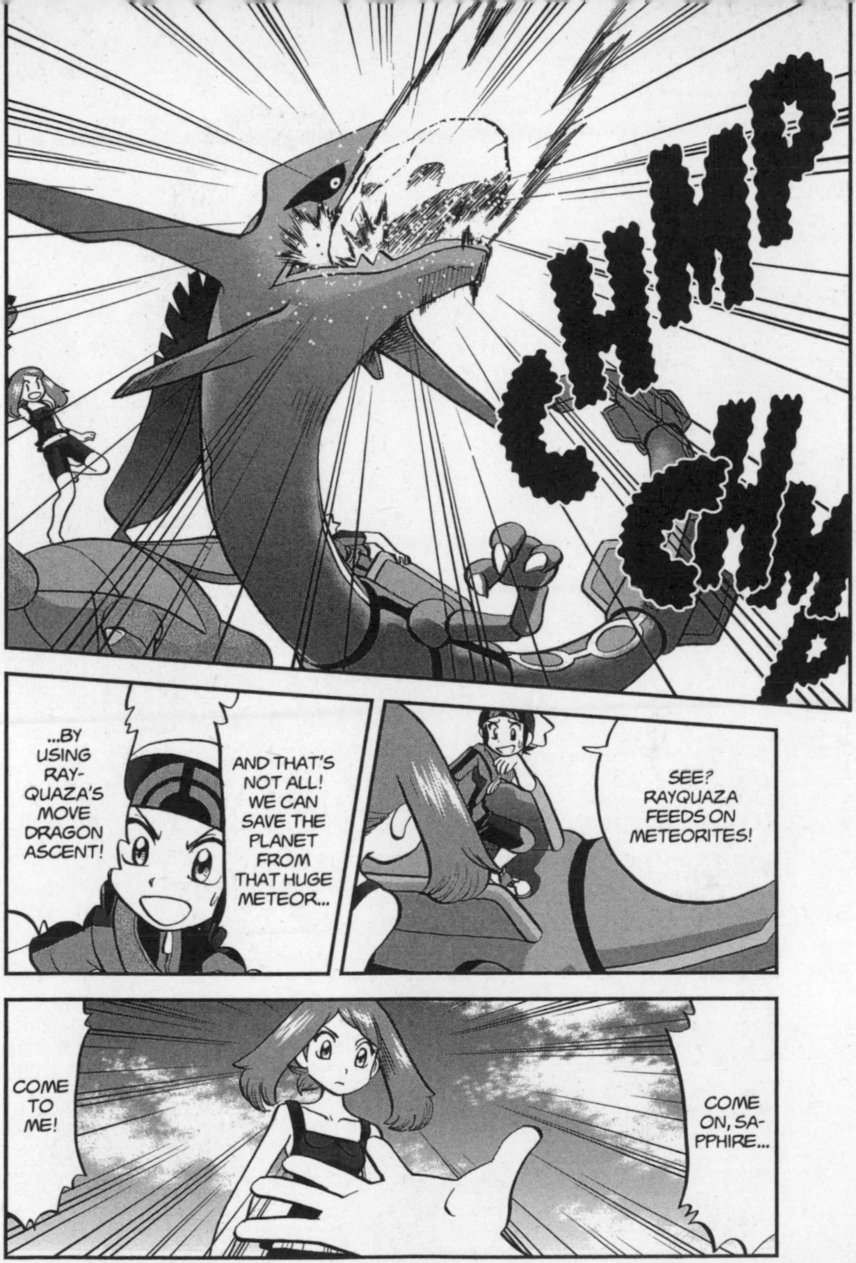
CHMP
CHMP
SEE? RAYQUAZA FEEDS ON METEORITES!
AND THAT'S NOT ALL! WE CAN SAVE THE PLANET FROM THAT HUGE METEOR...
...BY USING RAY-QUAZA'S MOVE DRAGON ASCENT!
COME ON, SA-PPHIRE...
COME TO ME!

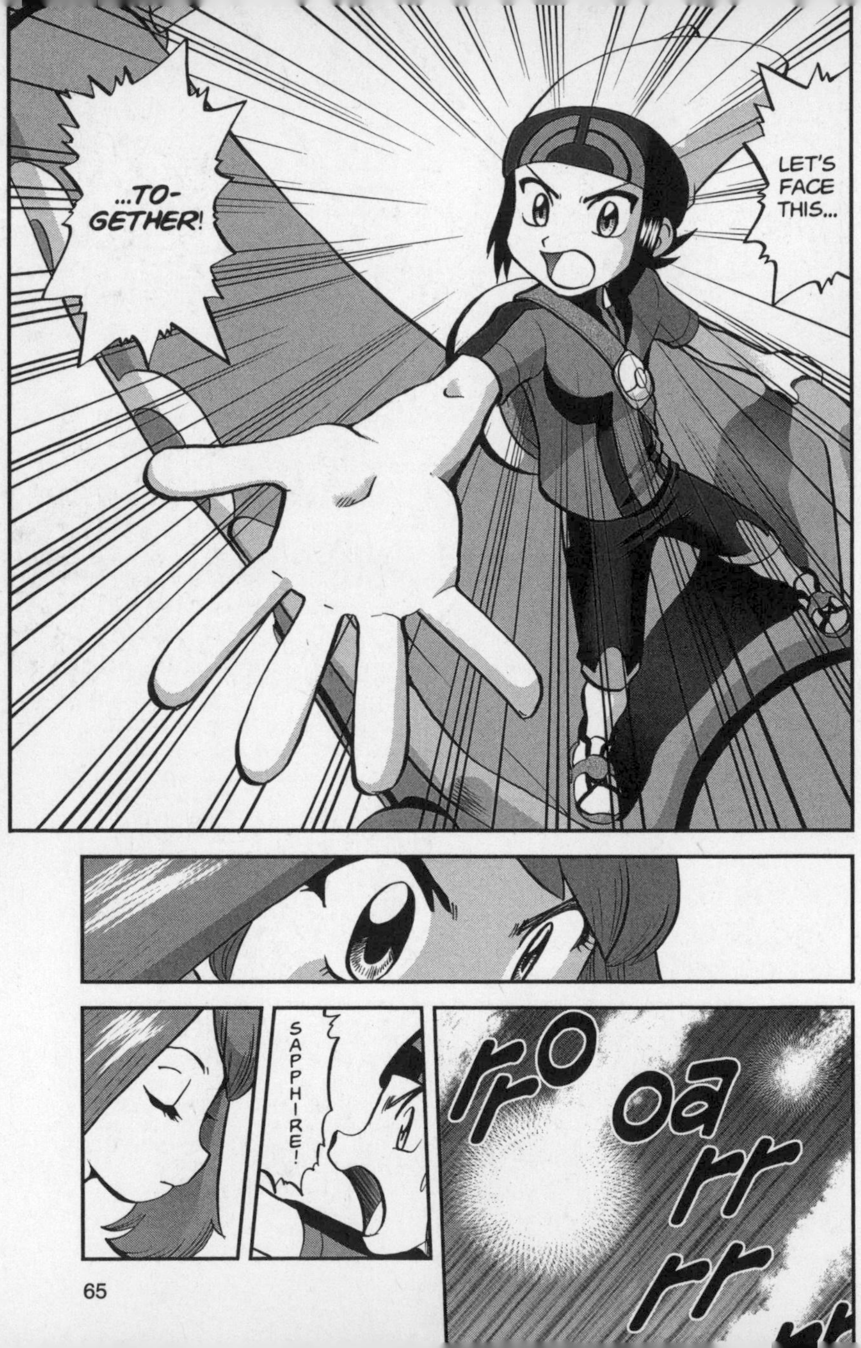
LET'S FACE THIS...
...TO-GETHER!
rooarrrr
SAPPHIRE!

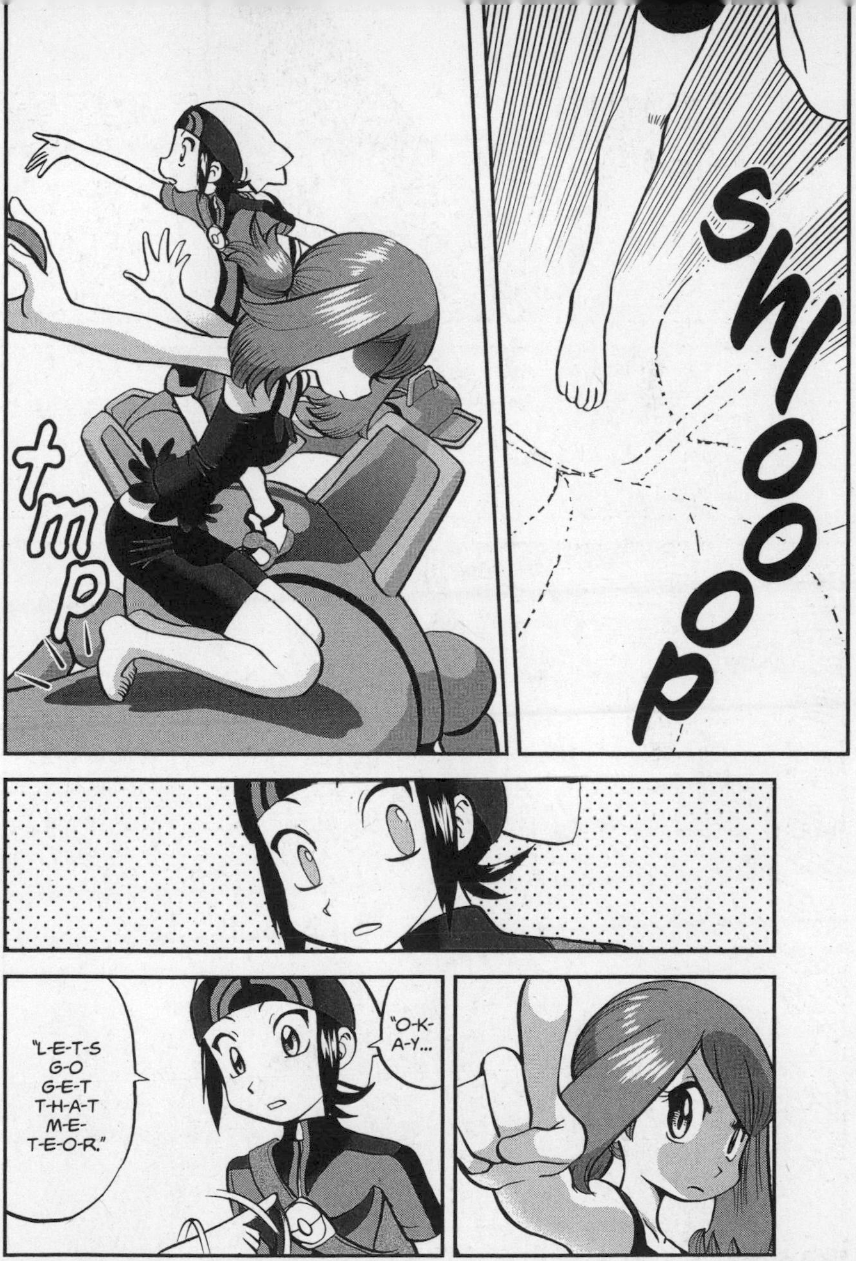
SHWOOOOP
tmp
"O-K-A-Y...
"L-E-T-S G-O G-E-T T-H-A-T M-E-T-E-O-R."

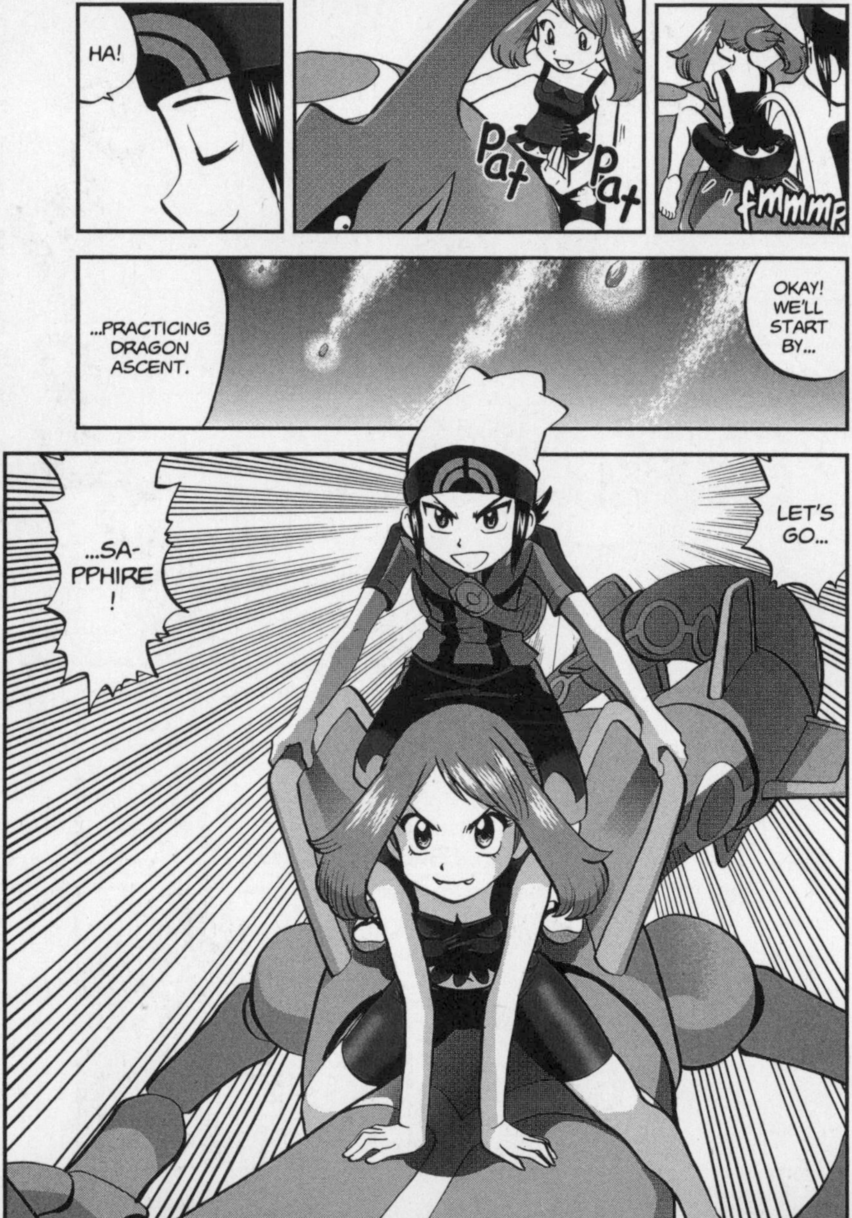
FMMMP
PAT PAT
HA!
OKAY! WE'LL START BY...
...PRACTICING DRAGON ASCENT.
LET'S GO...
...SA-PPHIRE!

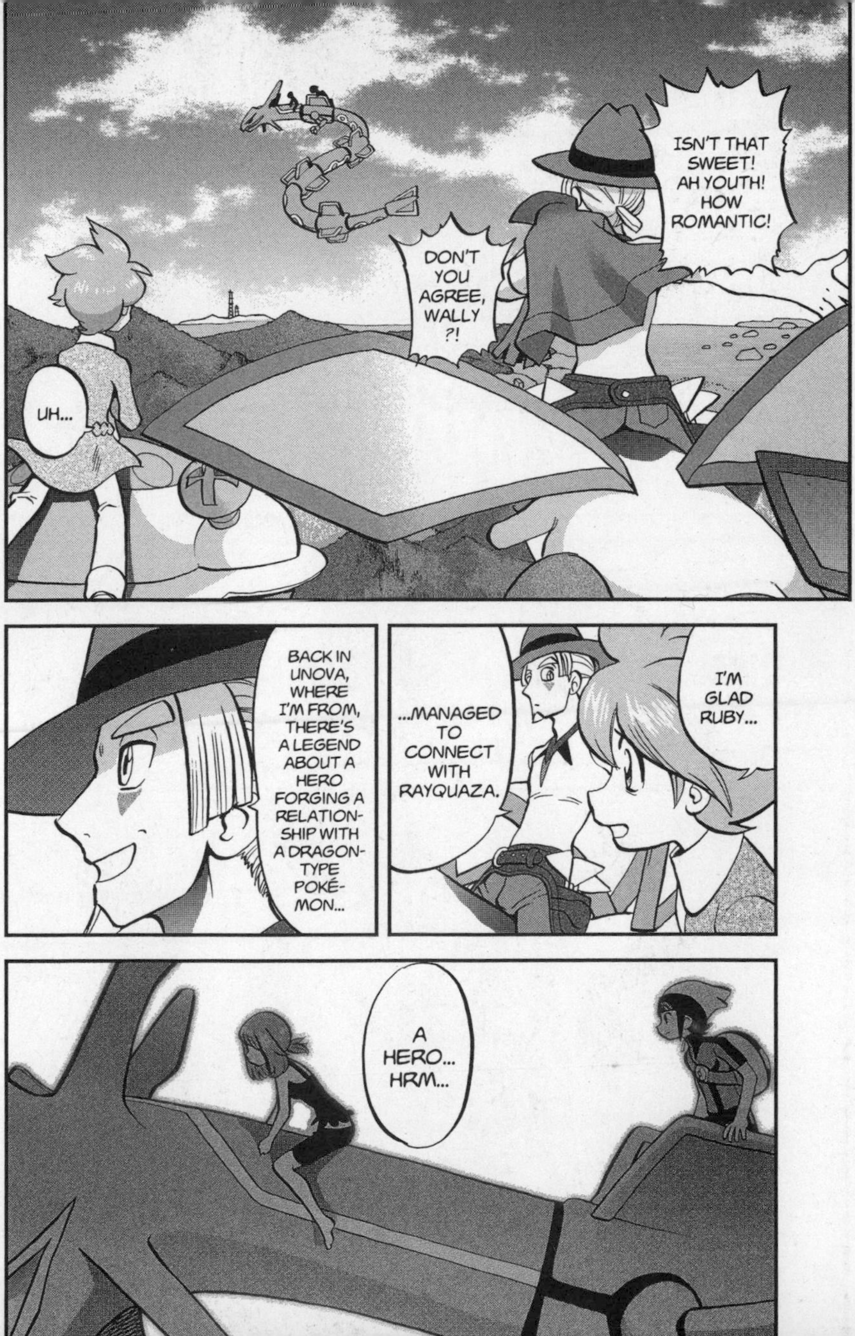
ISN'T THAT SWEET! AH YOUTH! HOW ROMANTIC!
DON'T YOU AGREE, WALLY ?!
UH...
I'M GLAD RUBY...
...MANAGED TO CONNECT WITH RAYQUAZA.
BACK IN UNOVA, WHERE I'M FROM, THERE'S A LEGEND ABOUT A HERO FORGING A RELATION-SHIP WITH A DRAGON-TYPE POKÉ-MON...
A HERO... HRM...

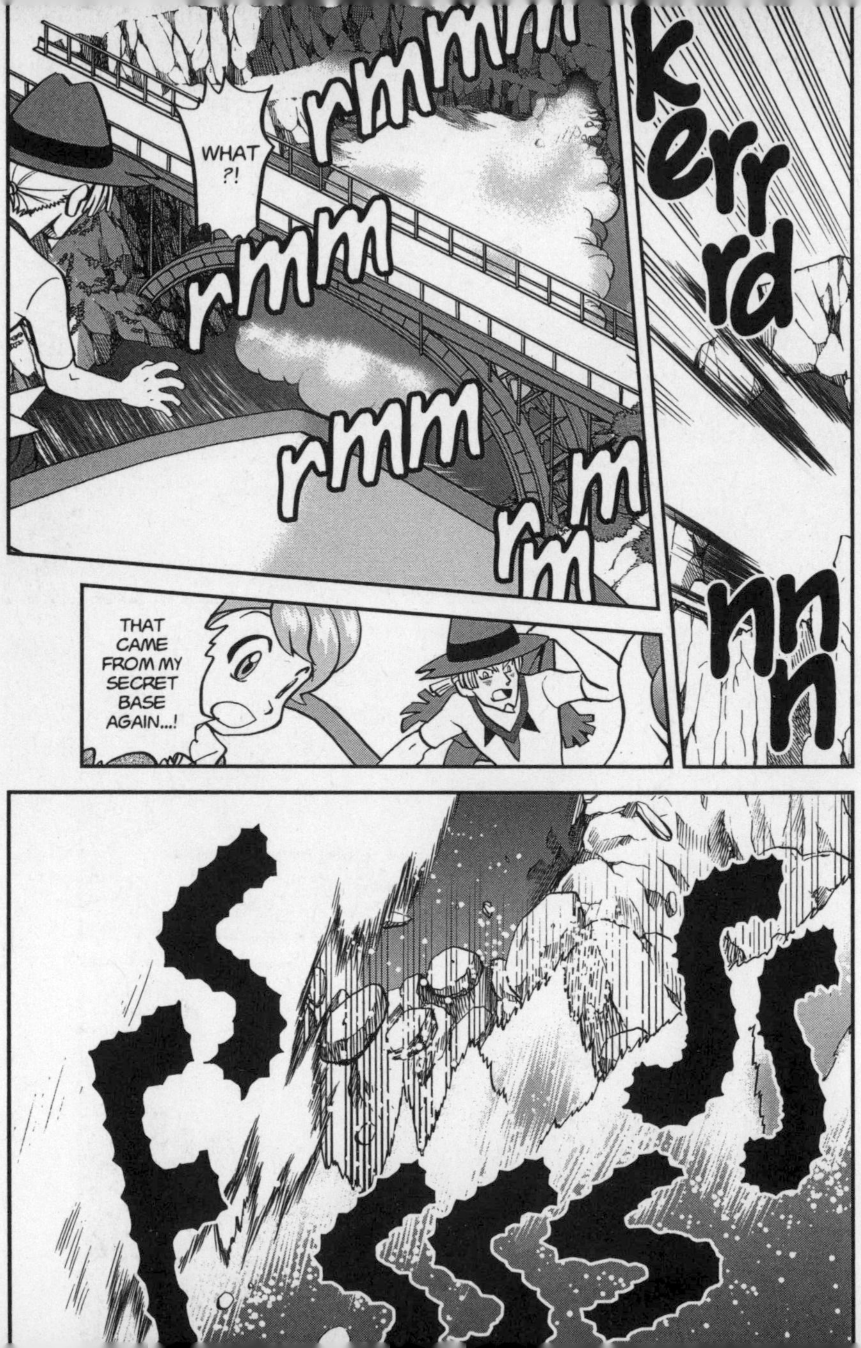
kerrrdnnn
WHAT?!
rmmm rmm rmm rm m rm
THAT CAME FROM MY SECRET BASE AGAIN...!

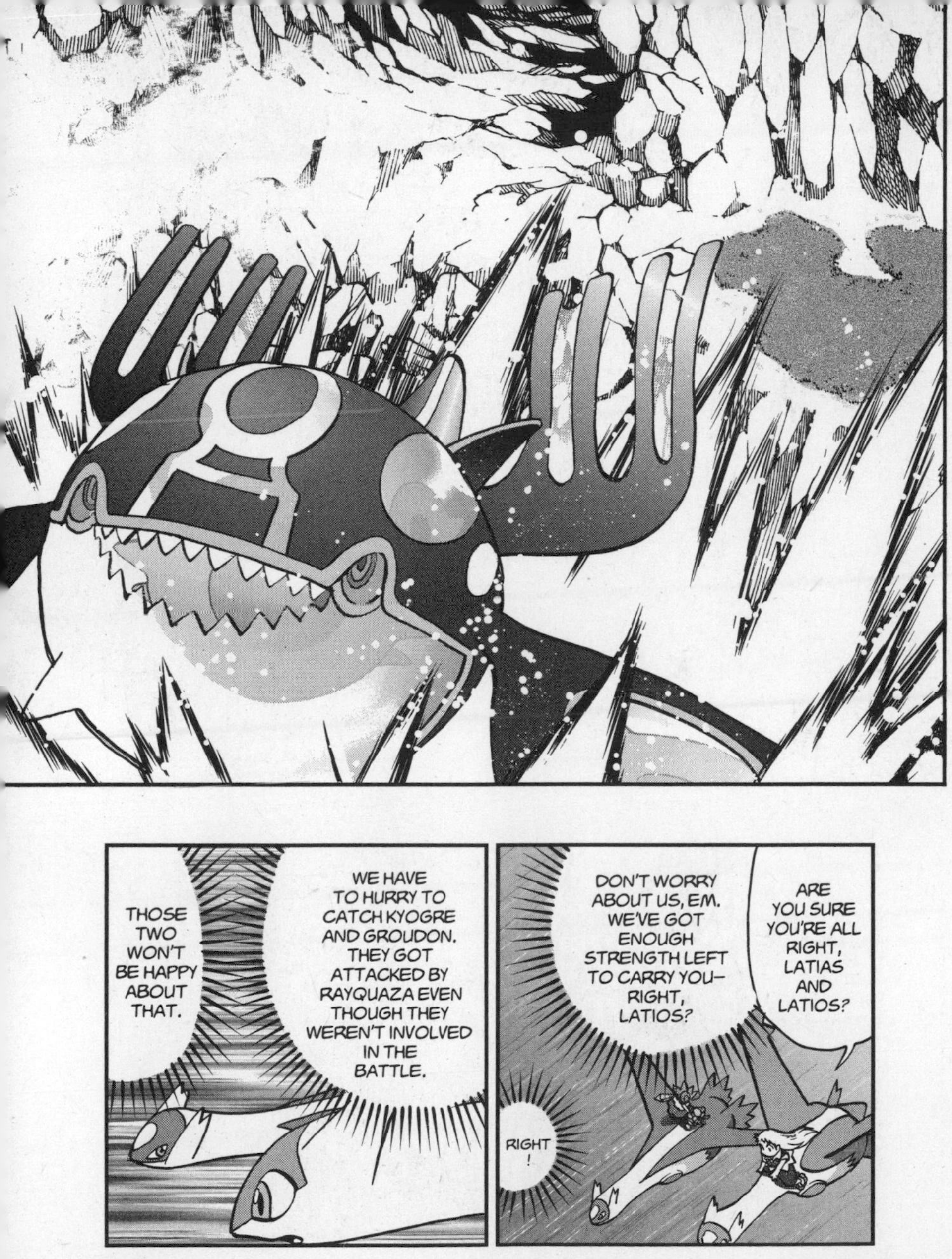
ARE YOU SURE YOU'RE ALL RIGHT, LATIAS AND LATIOS?
DON'T WORRY ABOUT US, EM. WE'VE GOT ENOUGH STRENGTH LEFT TO CARRY YOU–RIGHT, LATIOS?
RIGHT!
WE HAVE TO HURRY TO CATCH KYOGRE AND GROUDON. THEY GOT ATTACKED BY RAYQUAZA EVEN THOUGH THEY WEREN'T INVOLVED IN THE BATTLE.
THOSE TWO WON'T BE HAPPY ABOUT THAT.

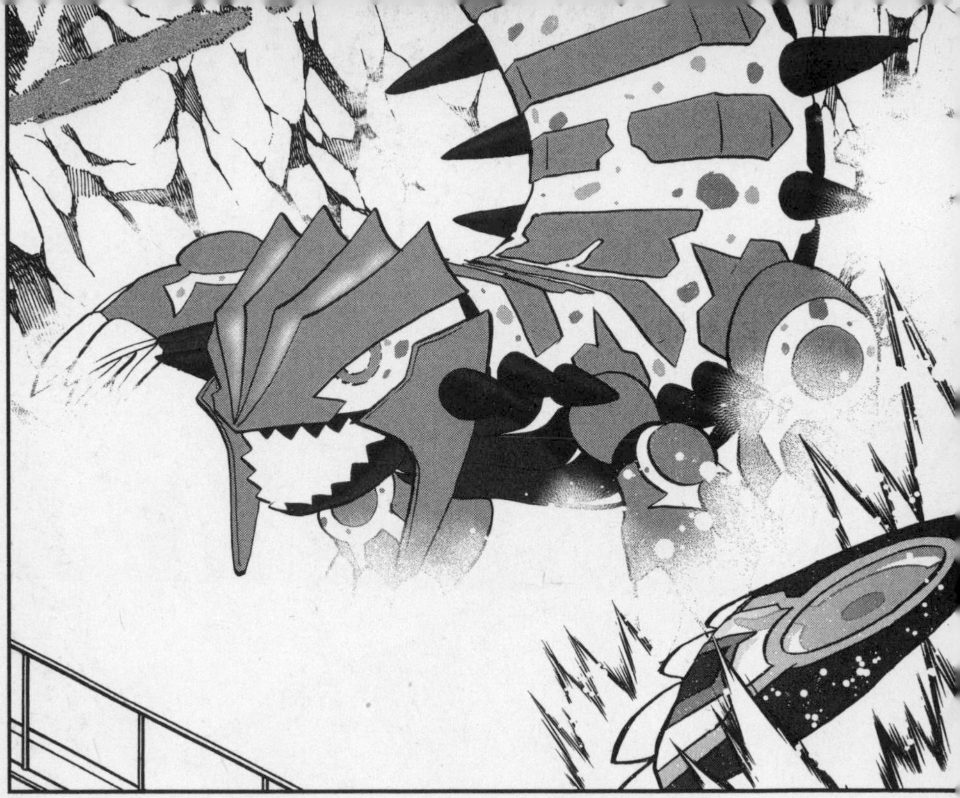

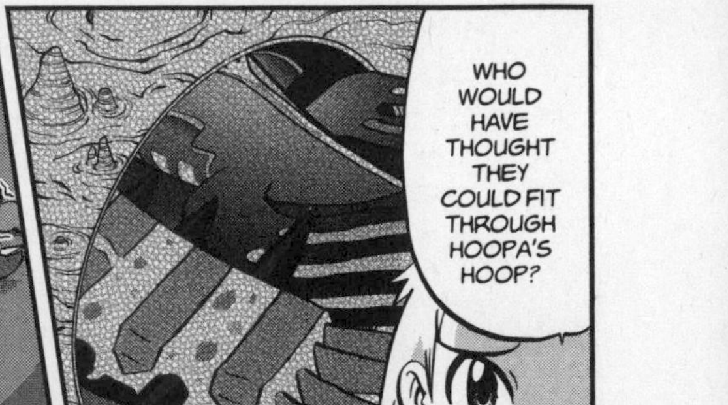
WHO WOULD HAVE THOUGHT THEY COULD FIT THROUGH HOOPA'S HOOP?

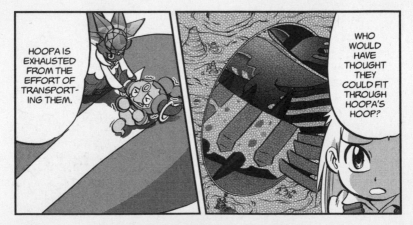

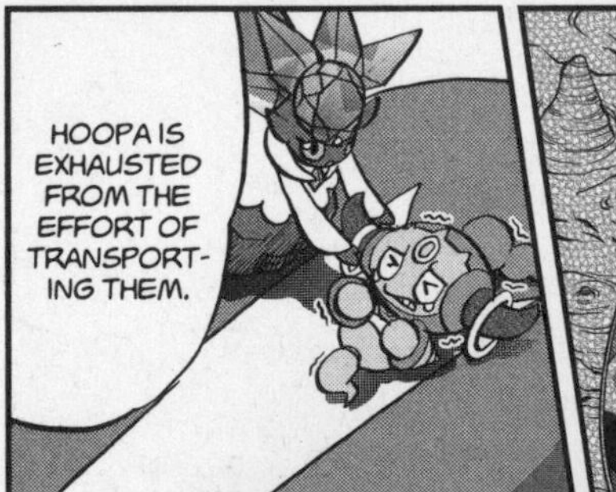
HOOPA IS EXHAUSTED FROM THE EFFORT OF TRANSPORTING THEM.

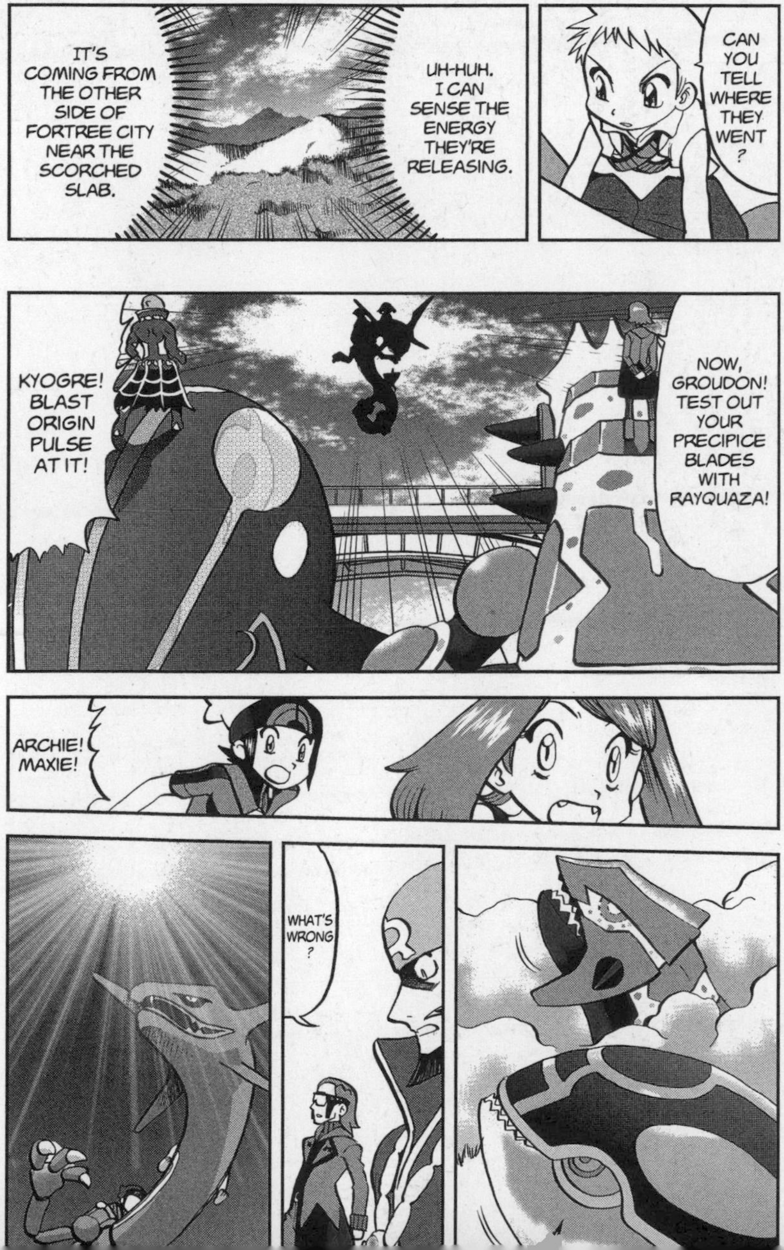
CAN YOU TELL WHERE THEY WENT?
UH-HUH. I CAN SENSE THE ENERGY THEY'RE RELEASING.
IT'S COMING FROM THE OTHER SIDE OF FORTREE CITY NEAR THE SCORCHED SLAB.
NOW, GROUDON! TEST OUT YOUR PRECIPICE BLADES WITH RAYQUAZA!
KYOGRE! BLAST ORIGIN PULSE AT IT!
ARCHIE! MAXIE!
WHAT'S WRONG?

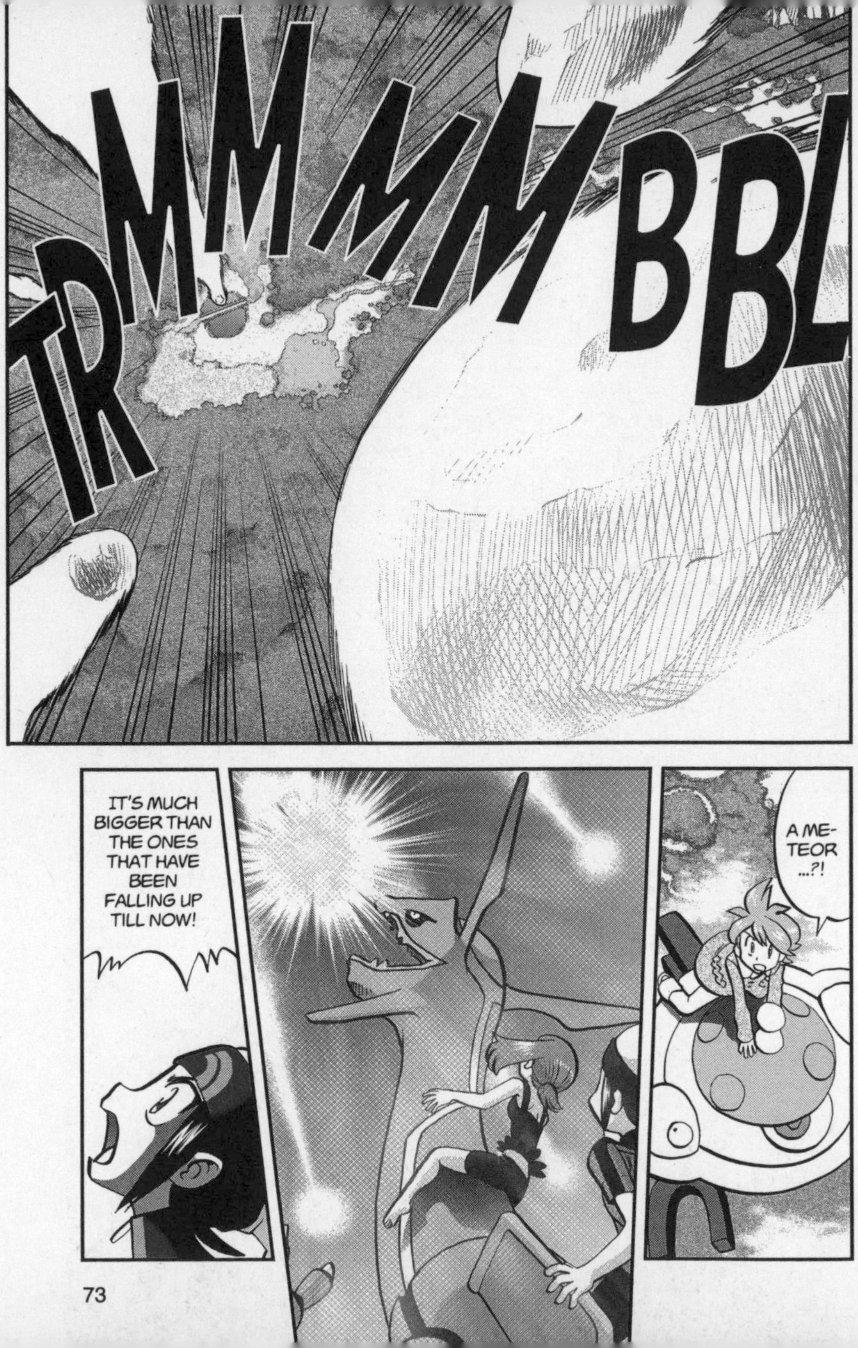
TRMMMMBBL
A ME-
TEOR
...?!
IT'S MUCH BIGGER THAN THE ONES THAT HAVE BEEN FALLING UP TILL NOW!

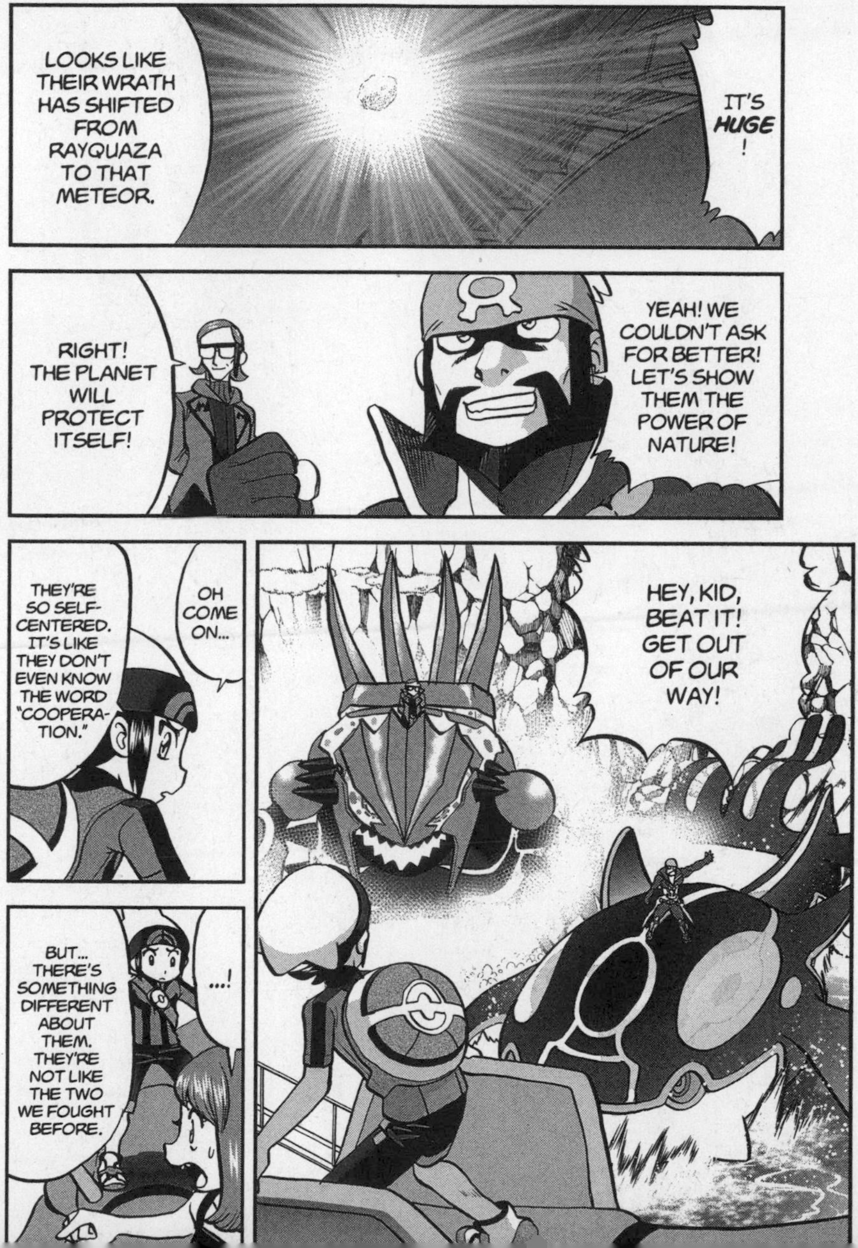
IT'S **HUGE**!
LOOKS LIKE THEIR WRATH HAS SHIFTED FROM RAYQUAZA TO THAT METEOR.
YEAH! WE COULDN'T ASK FOR BETTER! LET'S SHOW THEM THE POWER OF NATURE!
RIGHT! THE PLANET WILL PROTECT ITSELF!
HEY, KID, BEAT IT! GET OUT OF OUR WAY!
OH COME ON...
THEY'RE SO SELF-CENTERED. IT'S LIKE THEY DON'T EVEN KNOW THE WORD "COOPERATION."
...!
BUT... THERE'S SOMETHING DIFFERENT ABOUT THEM. THEY'RE NOT LIKE THE TWO WE FOUGHT BEFORE.

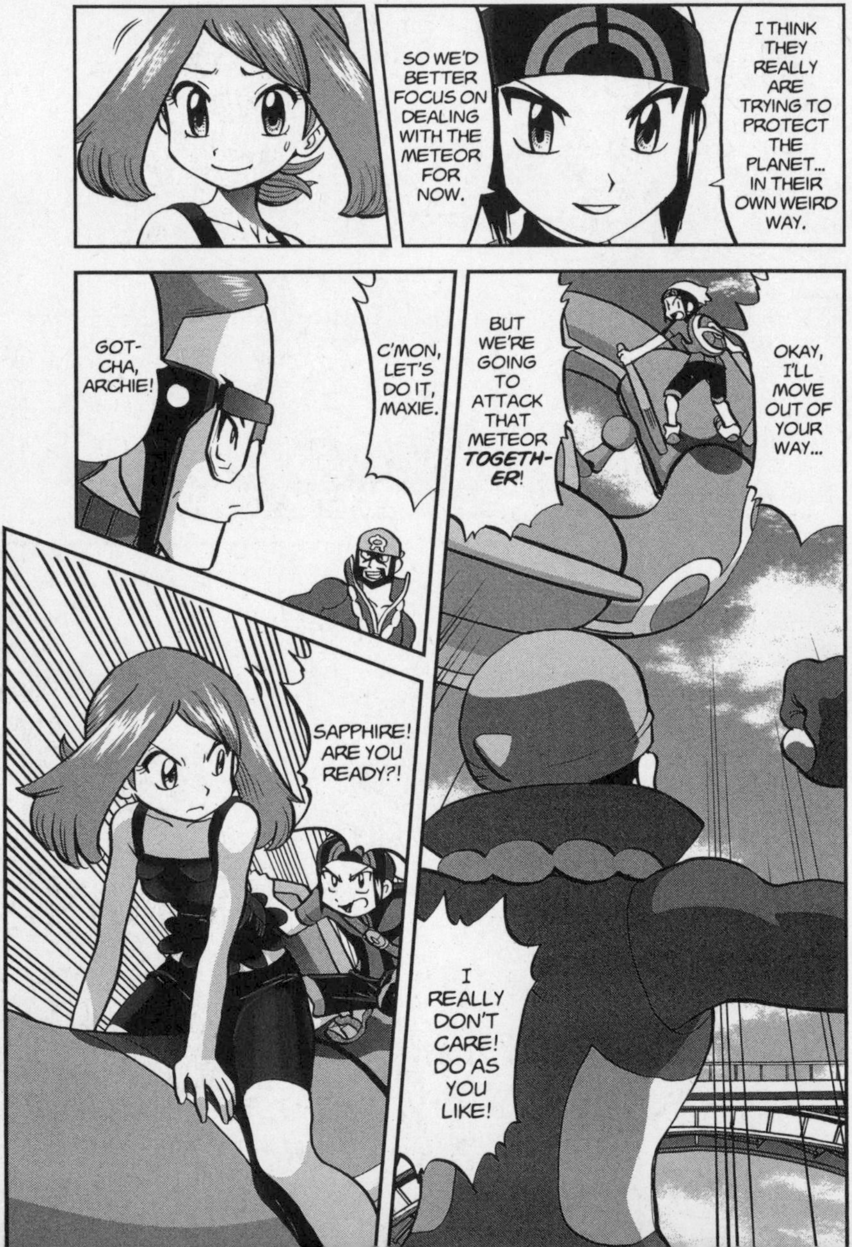

I THINK THEY REALLY ARE TRYING TO PROTECT THE PLANET... IN THEIR OWN WEIRD WAY.
SO WE'D BETTER FOCUS ON DEALING WITH THE METEOR FOR NOW.
OKAY, I'LL MOVE OUT OF YOUR WAY...
BUT WE'RE GOING TO ATTACK THAT METEOR ***TOGETH-ER***!
C'MON, LET'S DO IT, MAXIE.
GOT-CHA, ARCHIE!
SAPPHIRE! ARE YOU READY?!
I REALLY DON'T CARE! DO AS YOU LIKE!

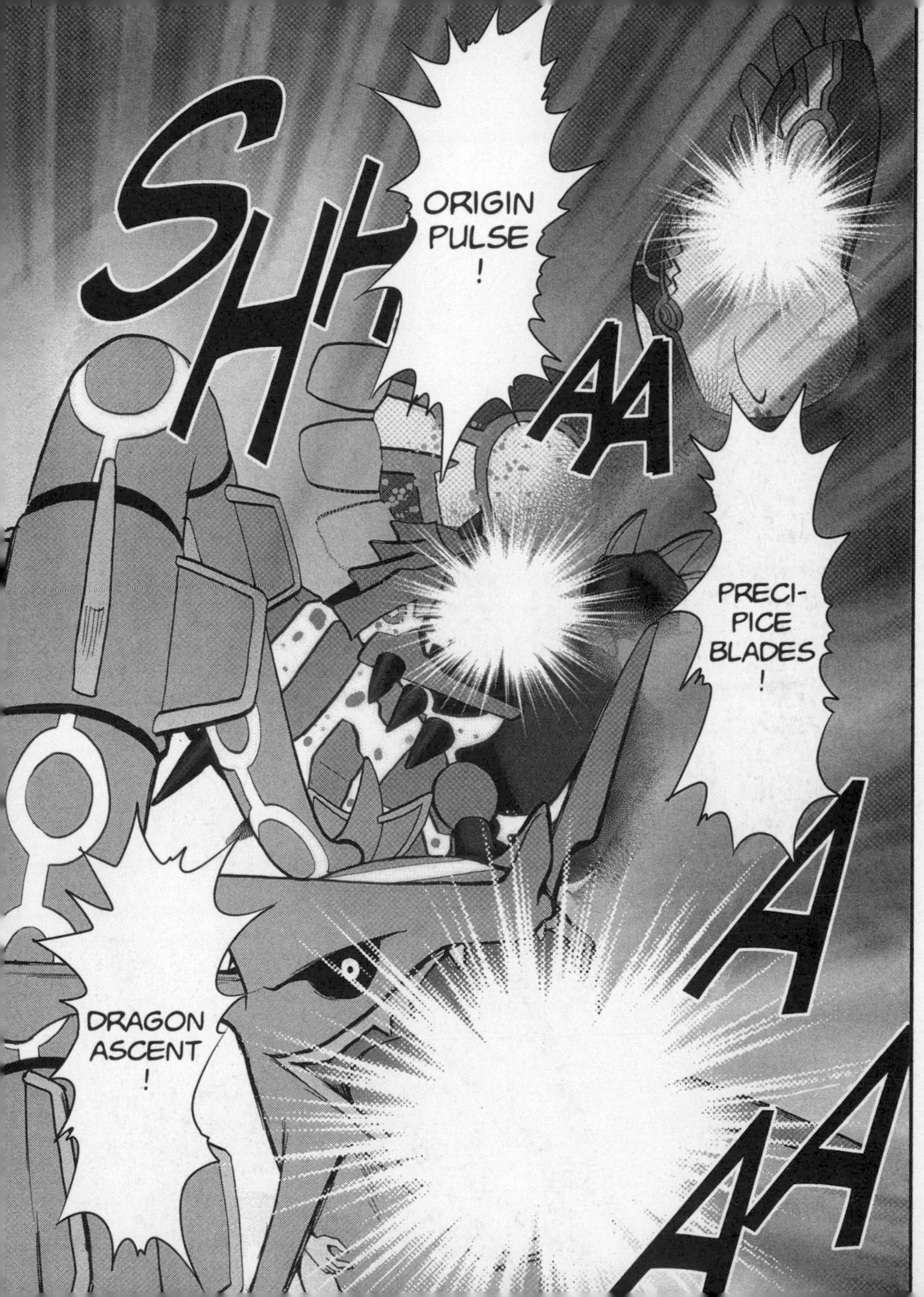
ORIGIN PULSE!
PRECI-PICE BLADES!
DRAGON ASCENT!
SHHAAAAAA

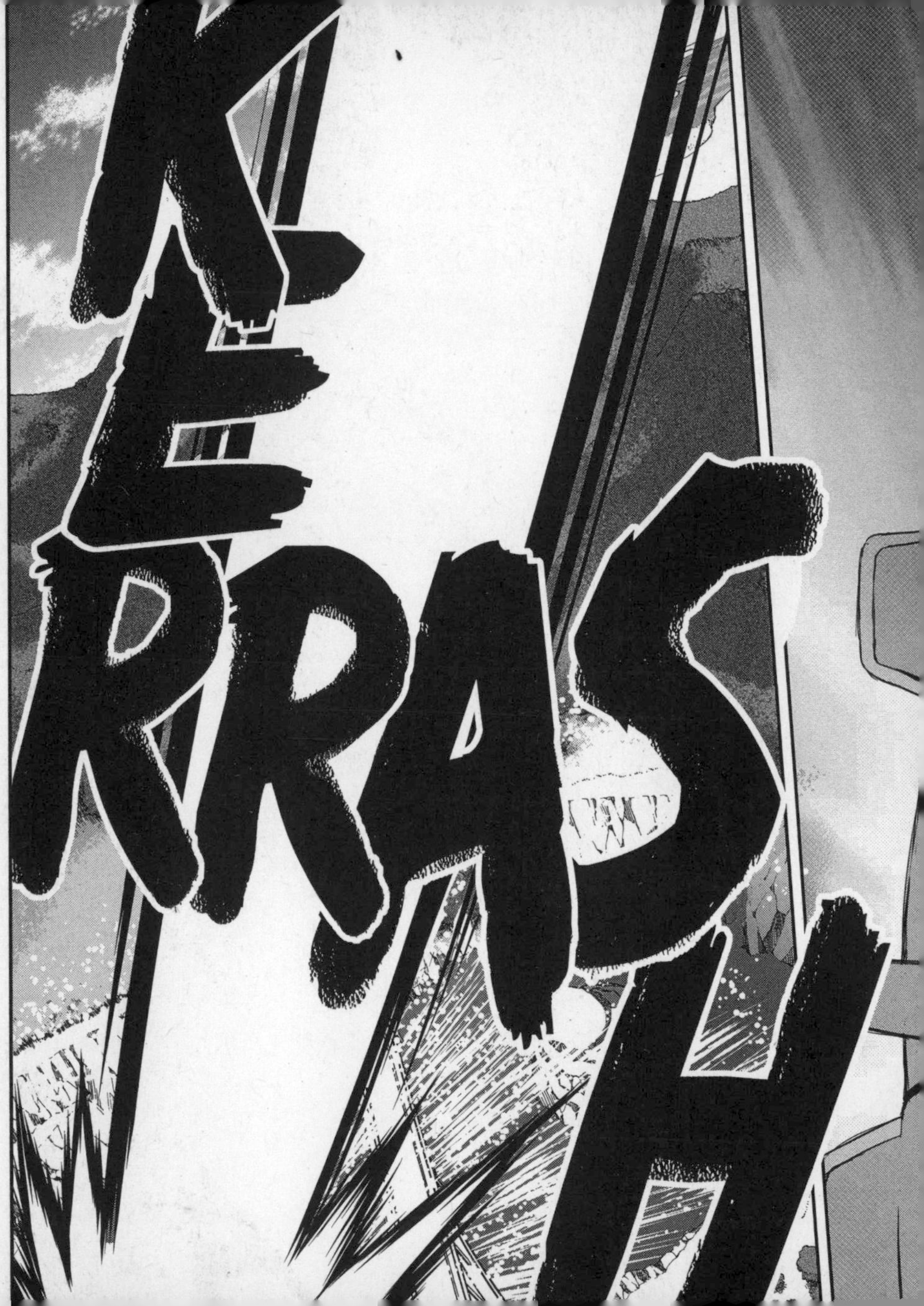
KERRASH

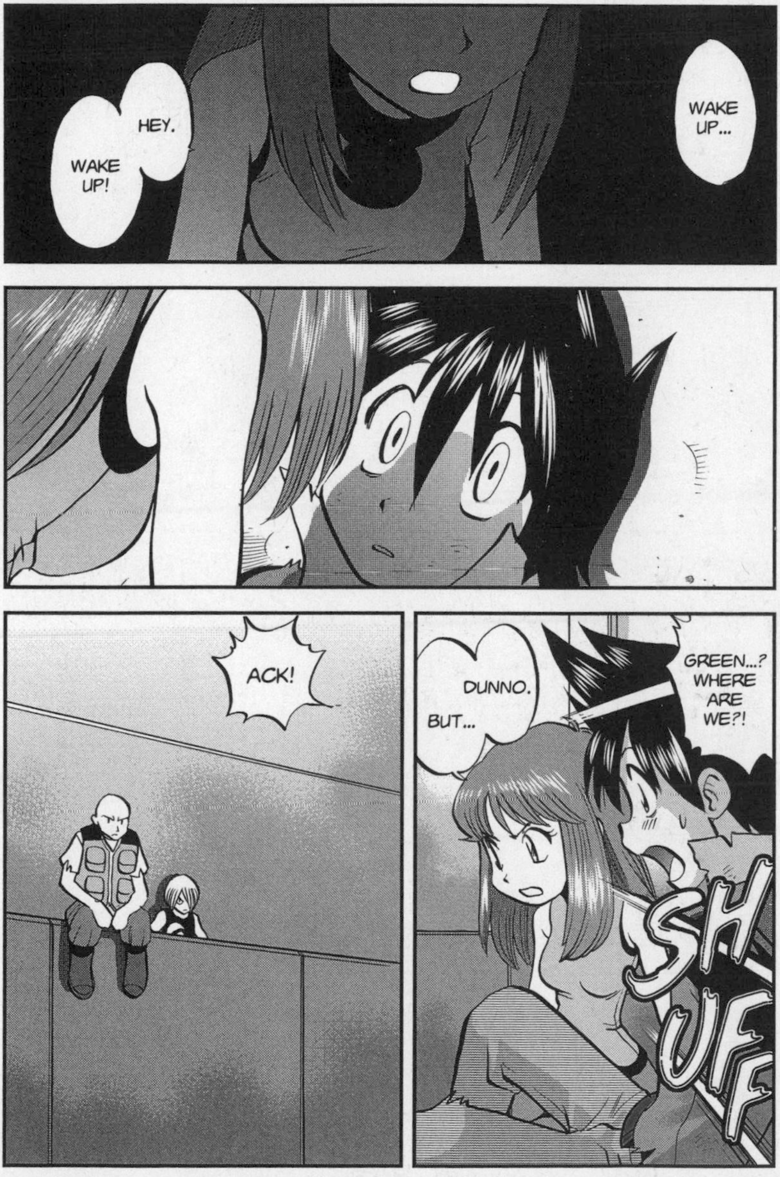
WAKE UP...
HEY.
WAKE UP!
GREEN...? WHERE ARE WE?!
DUNNO. BUT...
SHUFF
ACK!

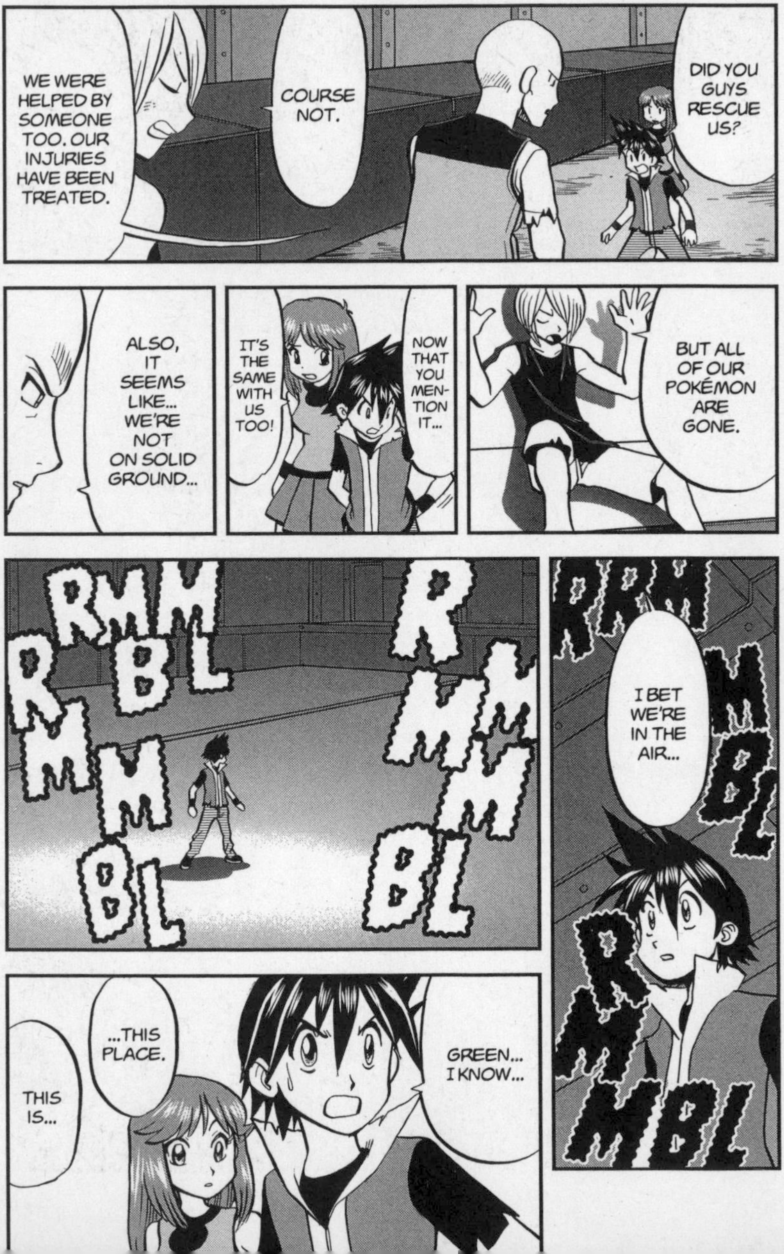
DID YOU GUYS RESCUE US?
COURSE NOT.
WE WERE HELPED BY SOMEONE TOO. OUR INJURIES HAVE BEEN TREATED.
BUT ALL OF OUR POKÉMON ARE GONE.
NOW THAT YOU MENTION IT...
IT'S THE SAME WITH US TOO!
ALSO, IT SEEMS LIKE... WE'RE NOT ON SOLID GROUND...
RRMMBL
I BET WE'RE IN THE AIR...
RRMMBL
RMMBL
RMMBL
GREEN... I KNOW...
...THIS PLACE.
THIS IS...

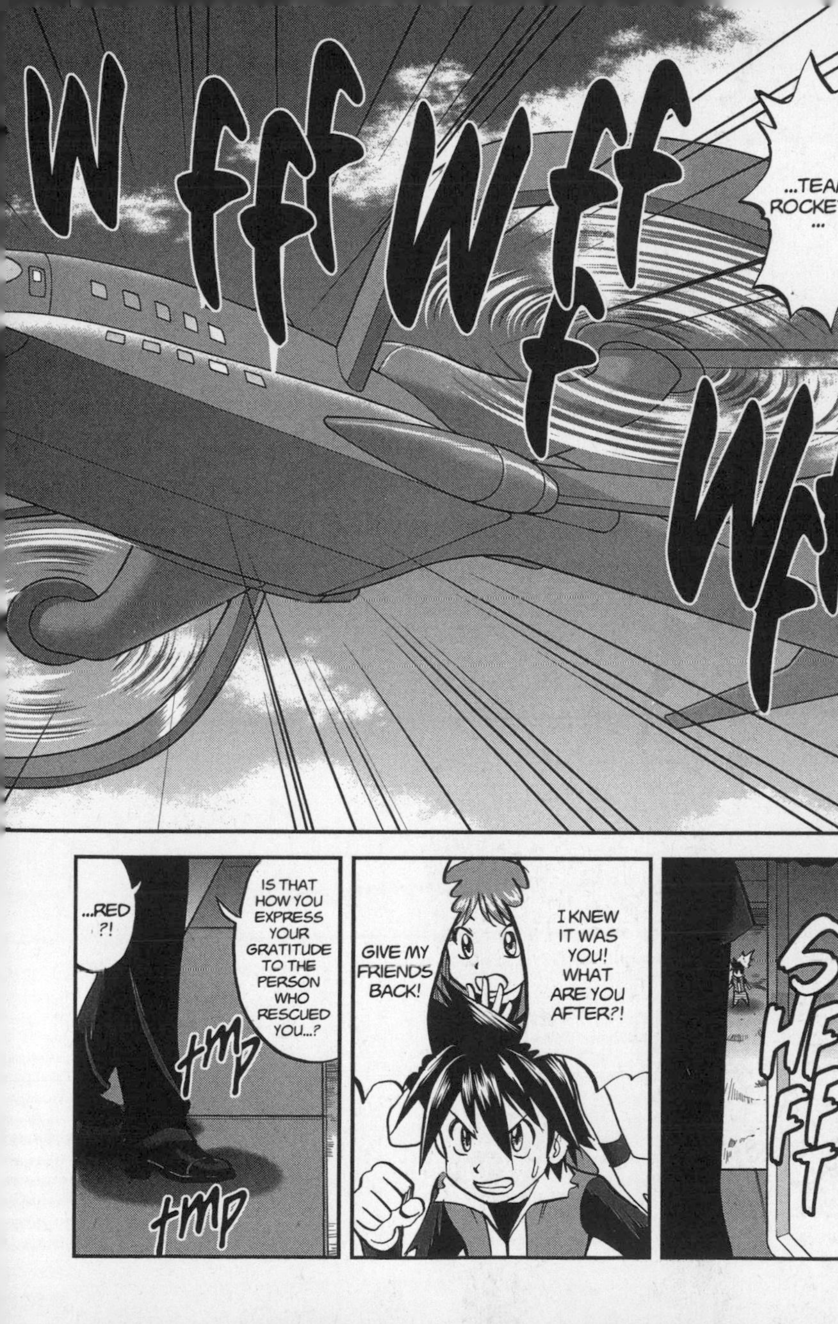
...TEAM ROCKET'S ...
WFFF WFFF WFFF
SHFFT
I KNEW IT WAS YOU! WHAT ARE YOU AFTER?!
GIVE MY FRIENDS BACK!
IS THAT HOW YOU EXPRESS YOUR GRATITUDE TO THE PERSON WHO RESCUED YOU...?
...RED ?!
TMP
TMP

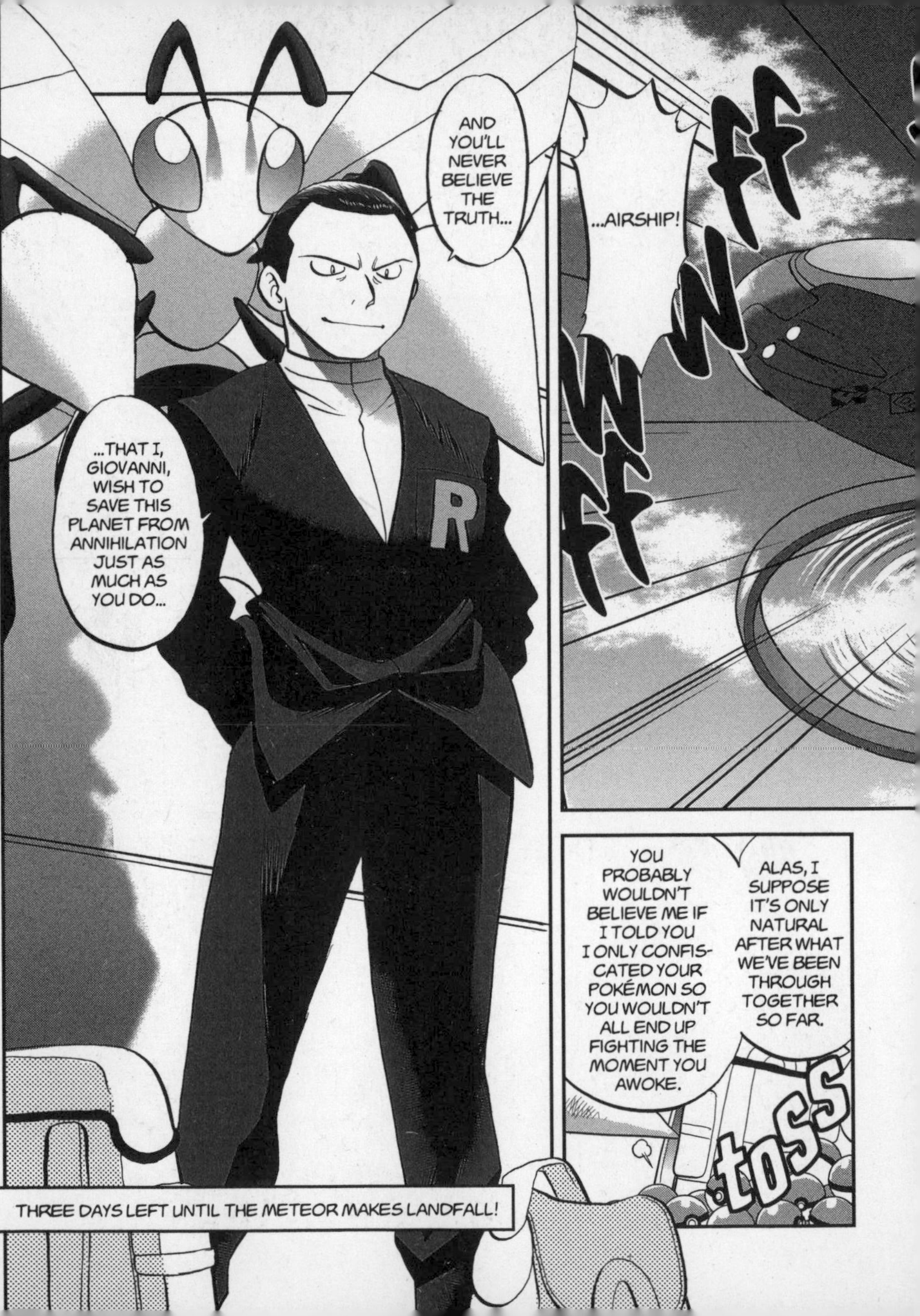
...AIRSHIP!
ALAS, I SUPPOSE IT'S ONLY NATURAL AFTER WHAT WE'VE BEEN THROUGH TOGETHER SO FAR.
YOU PROBABLY WOULDN'T BELIEVE ME IF I TOLD YOU I ONLY CONFIS-CATED YOUR POKÉMON SO YOU WOULDN'T ALL END UP FIGHTING THE MOMENT YOU AWOKE.
toss
AND YOU'LL NEVER BELIEVE THE TRUTH...
...THAT I, GIOVANNI, WISH TO SAVE THIS PLANET FROM ANNIHILATION JUST AS MUCH AS YOU DO...
THREE DAYS LEFT UNTIL THE METEOR MAKES LANDFALL!

PRECIPICE BLADES/ ORIGIN PULSE

Precipice Blades will turn the power of the land into the shape of a blade to attack the opponent. Origin Pulse will attack the opponent using numerous deep and brilliant blue lasers. They are unique moves that only Groudon and Kyogre can use. These moves, along with Primal Reversion, were Maxie and Archie's trump card against the meteor. The two trained in the deep cave of Meteor Falls with the permission of the Elder.

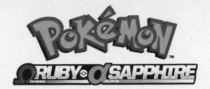

**Pokémon ΩRuby • αSapphire
Volume 5
VIZ Media Edition**

Story by HIDENORI KUSAKA
Art by SATOSHI YAMAMOTO

©2017 The Pokémon Company International.
©1995–2016 Nintendo / Creatures Inc. / GAME FREAK inc.
TM, ®, and character names are trademarks of Nintendo.
POCKET MONSTERS SPECIAL ΩRUBY • αSAPPHIRE Vol. 3
by Hidenori KUSAKA, Satoshi YAMAMOTO
© 2015 Hidenori KUSAKA, Satoshi YAMAMOTO
All rights reserved.
Original Japanese edition published by SHOGAKUKAN.
English translation rights in the United States of America, Canada, the
United Kingdom, Ireland, Australia, New Zealand and India arranged with
SHOGAKUKAN.

Translation—Tetsuichiro Miyaki
English Adaptation—Bryant Turnage
Touch-Up & Lettering—Susan Daigle-Leach
Design—Julian [JR] Robinson
Editor—Annette Roman

The stories, characters and incidents mentioned
in this publication are entirely fictional.

No portion of this book may be reproduced or transmitted
in any form or by any means without written permission
from the copyright holders.

Printed in the U.S.A.

Published by
VIZ Media, LLC
P.O. Box 77010
San Francisco, CA 94107

10 9 8 7 6 5 4 3 2 1
First printing, November 2017

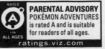

PARENTAL ADVISORY
POKÉMON ADVENTURES
is rated A and is suitable
for readers of all ages.
ratings.viz.com

www.viz.com

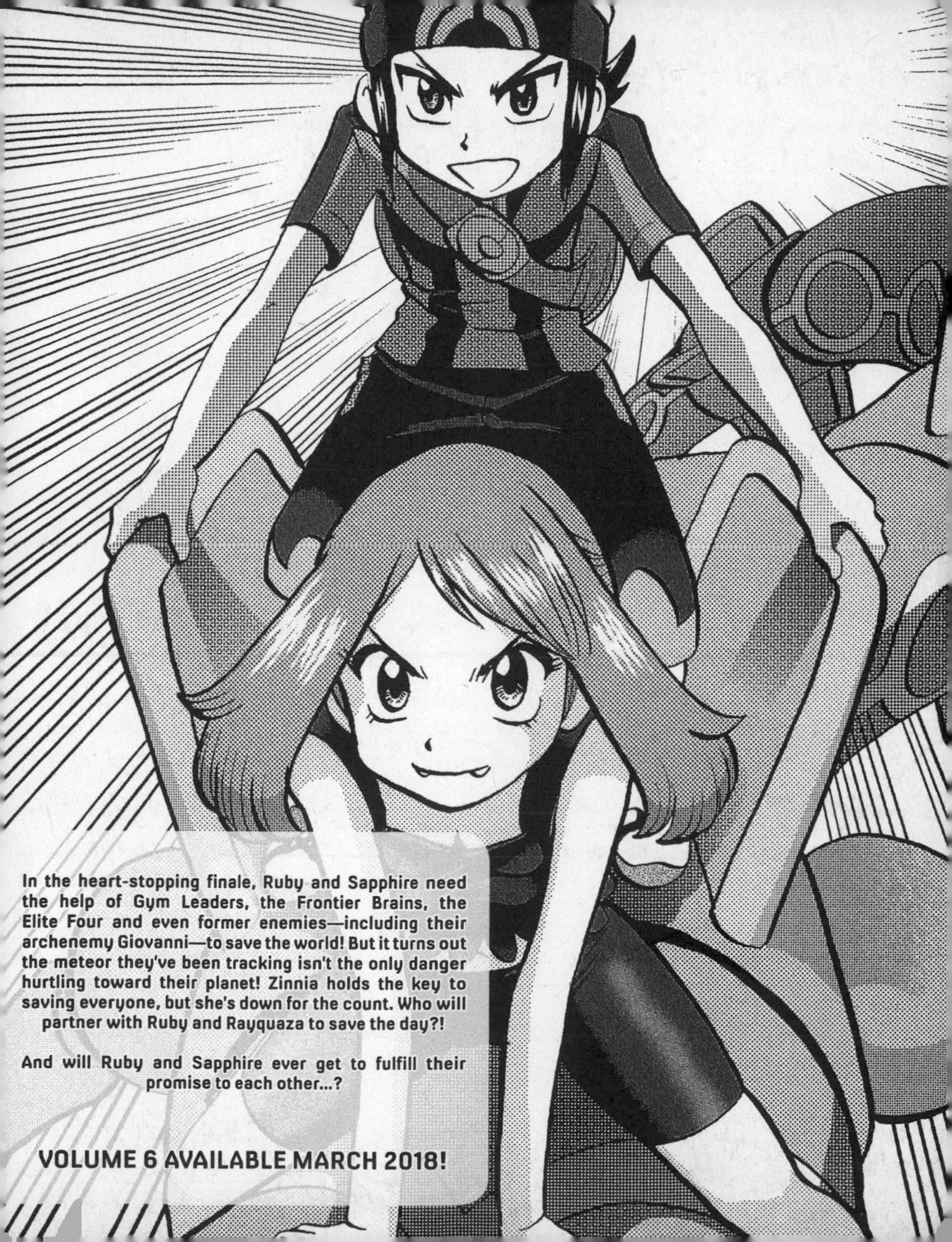

In the heart-stopping finale, Ruby and Sapphire need the help of Gym Leaders, the Frontier Brains, the Elite Four and even former enemies—including their archenemy Giovanni—to save the world! But it turns out the meteor they've been tracking isn't the only danger hurtling toward their planet! Zinnia holds the key to saving everyone, but she's down for the count. Who will partner with Ruby and Rayquaza to save the day?!

And will Ruby and Sapphire ever get to fulfill their promise to each other...?

VOLUME 6 AVAILABLE MARCH 2018!

Begin your Pokémon Adventure here in the Kanto region!

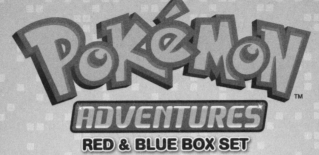

RED & BLUE BOX SET
Story by HIDENORI KUSAKA   **Art by MATO**

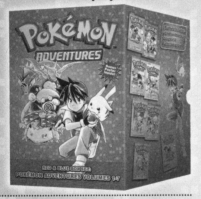

Includes POKÉMON ADVENTURES Vols. 1-7 and a collectible poster!

All your favorite Pokémon game characters jump out of the screen into the pages of this action-packed manga!

Red doesn't just want to train Pokémon, he wants to be their friend too. Bulbasaur and Poliwhirl seem game. But independent Pikachu won't be so easy to win over!

And watch out for Team Rocket, Red... They only want to be your enemy!

Start the adventure today!

© 2009-2012 Pokémon
© 1995-2010 Nintendo/Creatures Inc./GAME FREAK inc.
TM, ®, and character names are trademarks of Nintendo.
POCKET MONSTERS SPECIAL © 1997 Hidenori KUSAKA, MATO/SHOGAKUKAN

www.viz.com

PERFECT SQUARE

ALL AGES
rating.viz.com

The adventure continues in the Johto region!

POKÉMON™

ADVENTURES™

GOLD & SILVER BOX SET

Includes POKÉMON ADVENTURES Vols. 8-14 and a collectible poster!

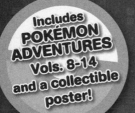

Story by HIDENORI KUSAKA

Art by MATO, SATOSHI YAMAMOTO

More exciting Pokémon adventures starring Gold and his rival Silver! First someone steals Gold's backpack full of Poké Balls (and Pokémon!). Then someone steals Prof. Elm's Totodile. Can Gold catch the thief—or thieves?!

Keep an eye on Team Rocket, Gold... Could they be behind this crime wave?

© 2010-2012 Pokémon
© 1995-2011 Nintendo/Creatures inc./GAME FREAK inc.
TM, ®, and character names are trademarks of Nintendo.
POCKET MONSTERS SPECIAL © 1997 Hidenori KUSAKA, MATO/SHOGAKUKAN
POCKET MONSTERS SPECIAL © 1997 Hidenori KUSAKA, Satoshi YAMAMOTO/SHOGAKUKAN

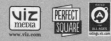

VIZ media www.viz.com

PERFECT SQUARE

RATED ALL AGES rating.viz.com

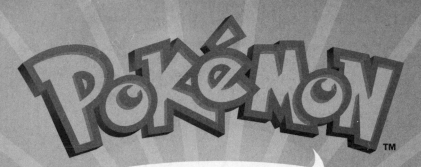

POCKET COMICS

STORY & ART BY **SANTA HARUKAZE**

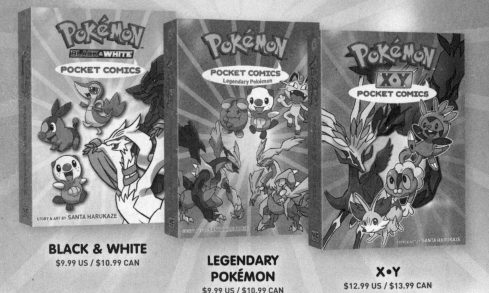

BLACK & WHITE
$9.99 US / $10.99 CAN

LEGENDARY POKÉMON
$9.99 US / $10.99 CAN

X•Y
$12.99 US / $13.99 CAN

A Pokémon pocket-sized book chock-full of four-panel gags, Pokémon trivia and fun quizzes based on the characters you know and love!

©2016 Pokémon.
©1995-2016 Nintendo/Creatures Inc./GAME FREAK inc. TM, ®, and character names are trademarks of Nintendo.
POKÉMON BW (Black • White) BAKUSHO 4KOMA MANGA ZENSHU © 2011 Santa HARUKAZE/SHOGAKUKAN
BAKUSHO 4KOMA DENSETSU NO POKÉMON O SAGASE!! © 2013 Santa HARUKAZE/SHOGAKUKAN
POKÉMON X•Y BAKUSHO 4KOMA MANGA ZENSHU © 2014 Santa HARUKAZE/SHOGAKUKAN

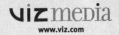
www.viz.com

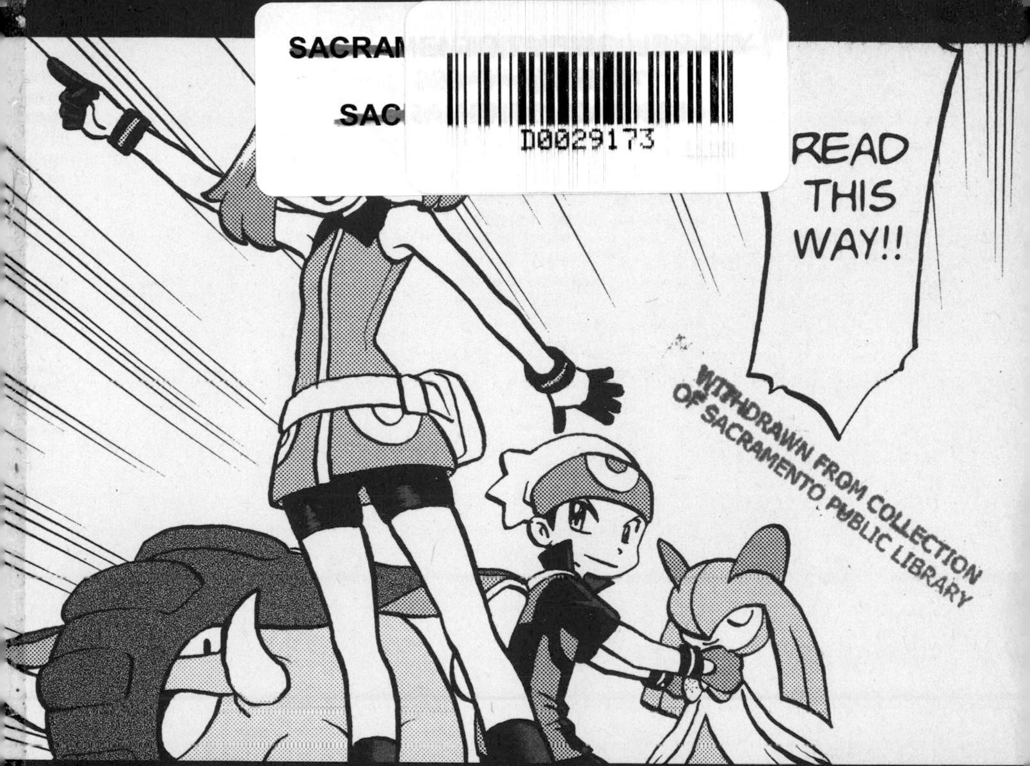
READ THIS WAY!!

THIS IS THE END OF THIS GRAPHIC NOVEL!

To properly enjoy this VIZ Media graphic novel, please turn it around and begin reading from right to left.

This book has been printed in the original Japanese format in order to preserve the orientation of the original artwork. Have fun with it!

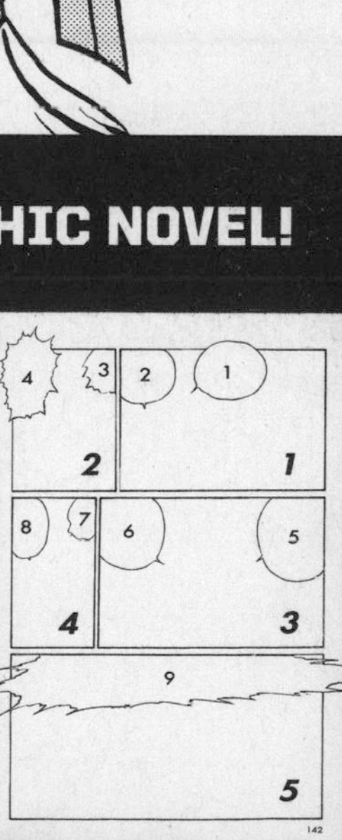

Follow the action this way.